The Forever Weekend

L.P. Maxa

ALSO BY L.P. MAXA

RiffRaff Records

Royalty

Legacy

Infamy

Loyalty

Sanctuary

Piracy

Certainty

Inevitably

Finally

The Devil's Share

Play Nice

Play Dirty

Play Fair

Play Softly

Play Hard

Play For Keeps

St. Leasing

Mouth Watering

Breath Taking

Jaw Dropping

Heart Stopping

Soul Crushing

Other Novels

Happy Place

Stumbled into Love

Rescued

www.BOROUGHSPUBLISHINGGROUP.com

THE FOREVER WEEKEND

ISBN: 978-1-951055-95-0

To all those laughter-filled nights we can never talk about again

ACKNOWLEDGMENTS

Before the recent additions and changes, this book had been titled *Never Ever*, and I wrote it after a girls' trip to the beach with a group of my friends. They were my inspiration then, and they're my support now. So this time, I want to thank all my wonderful girlfriends. Thank you for all the laughter and the dancing. Thank you for the late night What-a-Burger runs and the perfectly made cocktails. Thank you for the road trips and the inside jokes. Thank you for the drawer full of custom t-shirts. Thank you for knowing all my secrets. Thank you for giving me memories to last a lifetime.

The Forever Weekend

*"A good friend knows all your stories.
A best friend helped you write them."*
—Unknown

Prologue

Livi

I pulled my sporty little Audi into an empty parking spot at my husband's swanky downtown office. It'd been ages since I'd visited him at work. "Kasey, I'm going to have to call you back." I held the phone against my ear with my shoulder and shut the car door with my foot.

"No. We have to get these tickets booked *today,* Livi."

I rolled my eyes as I tried to balance the bags of takeout I was carrying and my oversized purse. "I'm surprising Patrick with lunch, and my hands are full. I'm going to end up dropping my phone."

"You'll be fine."

I took and let out a deep calming breath. "Fine, give me a second to readjust." I didn't wait for her reply before setting my phone on the hood of my car and transferring all the bags into one hand. "Okay. Now, tell me the flying death trap times again." Half-heartedly, I listened to my best friend list the departure times for our upcoming trip to Georgia as I balanced all my crap and headed through the spinning doors to surprise my husband with his favorite meal.

I felt like we'd been growing apart lately, and the distance had finally gotten to me. We were both so busy, and we seemed to be on two completely different schedules. He got home late, and I left the house early. Weekends were full of obligations with friends and to-do lists a mile long. I'd woken up that morning, feeling so far away from my husband that there was a slight ache in my chest. I needed to make more of an effort to put our marriage first. I knew that if I did, Patrick would follow suit. He was a workaholic, but he loved me. I simply needed to remind him that I was still here.

"Is that good for you?"

My friend's question snapped me out of my head and reminded me that I was still on the phone. "I'm fine with whatever, Kasey. You're the one with the kid. We'll leave when it works for you."

I was super pumped for our yearly girls' trip, even if I wasn't really paying attention to the smaller details like flight times. I needed a vacay in the worst way. Ha. That rhymed, I could use it in my next book. I should write it down or I'd forget, my brain was a scattered mess on a good day. What were the chances I could grab my notebook out of my purse without dropping all the food and shattering my cell on the shiny waxed concrete? Probably not great, I shouldn't even attempt it.

When the elevator doors opened, I pressed the button to the top floor. Patrick was successful, and his office was proof. A lot of glass windows and modern leather, sterile if you asked me. Although no one had. Not even the annoyingly put-together interior designer his company had hired after his last promotion.

Miraculously, my cell hadn't dropped Kasey's call while I was riding to the eighteenth floor. I'd listened while she had discussed the pros and cons of flying out before or after her toddler's nap time. I loved her kid, with all my heart, but I needed her to pick a flight and let me have lunch with my husband in peace.

"Okay, I've really got to go now, Kasey, I'm walking up to his door." Usually Patrick's secretary was posted at her desk outside his office, but today it was empty. Oh. Duh, Mrs. Mitchell retired, he'd told me that weeks ago. I wondered if he hired someone new yet. Had he mentioned it to me and I'd let it go in one ear and out the other? I needed to make a better effort to listen about his day. It was so late by the time he got home, I was usually a glass of wine deep and mentally exhausted.

"Livi. Are you even listening to me?"

I snorted. "No, I'm *not* listening to you. I told you I need to go, my hands are full, and I'm two seconds away from walking into Patrick's office." I balanced the phone against my shoulder once again, using my free hand to open the oversize door. "Kasey, book the tickets and then email me the…Holy. Fuck."

"What? Holy fuck, what?"

I dropped the takeout bags, Mexican food exploded everywhere while my purse slid down to the floor beside my feet. The only thing I managed to keep a death grip on was my cell phone.

My husband was having sex with a tiny blonde woman. They were going at it on his desk so hard they didn't even hear me walk in. I mean it was a huge office, but still. They didn't hear me talking on the phone, or me dropping the food. They didn't hear my life crumbling before my eyes. Which was odd, because to me it sounded a lot like a fucking explosion.

"Livi? What's going on?"

"Patrick is having sex with someone on his desk," I whispered into the phone as I stood there, in the doorway to Patrick's coldly styled office, and watched him have sex with someone who wasn't me. Why was I whispering? It was as if I didn't want to interrupt them. Was she his new secretary? If so, she certainly had different job duties than seventy-year-old Mrs. Mitchell.

"What? Livi?"

"This is the most cliché moment of my entire life." I angled my head to the side, getting a better view. "I'll have to call you back. Love you, bye."

I couldn't quite decide how I felt in that instant. I kind of wanted to throw an epic fit, scream, and break all the overpriced things within my reach. Then again, I kind of wanted to turn around and let them finish. I tilted my head to the other side, watching him nail into her.

Patrick's pale white ass was on full display and the blonde's legs were spread so wide it looked like she was doing a split. Huh. I couldn't tell you the last time my husband had fucked me like that. For some reason, it was *that* thought that finally set me off.

"Are you fucking kidding me?"

Two heads swiveled in my direction, finally realizing that they weren't alone. It took them long enough. Pretty sure I'd been standing in the doorway for actual minutes. Patrick's eyes went as wide as those stupid china plates he insisted we register for, the ones I'd hated. He scrambled off the girl, pulling his slacks up from around his ankles.

"Livi. Shit, this isn't what it looks like."

I laughed, manically, like a crazy person. "For real? *This isn't what it looks like?* It *looks* like you are cheating on me." I threw my hands up, shrugging dramatically. "Am I confused? Is it something else?" I reached down and grabbed a foil-wrapped burrito from the pile of food on the floor, and then chucked it at his head. "Is it some kind of new Heimlich maneuver?" I got him in the shoulder, but the burrito basically imploded and his shirt was ruined so I was marginally happy. "Was she choking?"

The girl was now dressed and cowering in a corner. Her continued presence was only pissing me off further. Read the room, chick.

"No, honey, look… Shit. I am so sorry, Livi, please, honey—"

I cut him off when I tossed the entire cup of hot queso on his crotch. I smiled when he let out a rather high-pitched shriek, doubling over in pain. Stupid bastard. "Don't call me honey. Don't call me period. Don't text me. Don't come home. I mean it, Patrick. We're done."

"Livi, sweetie, you don't mean that. Let's talk about this. We can fix this."

He was simultaneously trying to keep the scalding cheese away from his dick and pleading with me to stay. His home-wrecker blonde was now crying in the corner. I didn't know why I kept focusing on the fact that she was a blonde. In reality, it didn't matter what color hair she had. She'd fucked my husband. We'd never be friends.

"There is nothing to fix. Asshole." I picked up my purse from the floor and frowned when I realized I'd thrown the only intact burrito. Cheating husband or not, a girl had to eat. "Not anymore," I huffed, slamming the door so hard on my way out that the windows rattled and every head on the floor swiveled in my direction. I felt this weird anger/numbness come over me as I made my way back to the elevators. Almost like I knew I should be furious, but part of me didn't give two flying fucks.

I thought work and our busy schedules were driving us apart. I'd felt guilty for not being a better wife, a better partner, but really it was Patrick's inability to keep his dick in his pants. I wondered how long he'd been cheating. I wondered if that was the first girl. I wondered if I called in another food order on my way to the car if it'd be ready in the time it'd take me to drive back to the restaurant.

I suddenly couldn't tell what I was more upset about. The fact that I walked in on my husband fucking someone else, or that I'd wasted all that amazing Mexican food.

Chapter One

Livi

Airplanes were not my most favorite place to be. They smelled bad and were a breeding ground for bacteria. Not to mention that heavy metal boxes had no business being in the air. But I'd calculated the drive to Georgia, and it wasn't worth it for a long weekend. So, I'd let my best friend drag my ass onto the unnatural monstrosity.

"Are you going to tell them?"

I shook my head as I collapsed into the thin blue leather seat. "Nope."

"You need to tell them."

I rolled my eyes, as I stored my purse in its proper place under my feet. "Yes, Kasey, I'm aware that I need to tell my best friends that I'm getting divorced."

"You should have told them when it happened."

I sighed; this was getting exasperating. Kasey had been giving me a hard time about keeping secrets ever since they called us for boarding. I'd never thought I'd be getting divorced. When I said *I do*, I had every intention of *I Doing* forever. It was more embarrassing than I expected, harder to talk about with the people close to me. I could ramble about my personal life to the grocery store bag boy, and I had, but I was finding it near impossible to open up to my friends.

"It's not so easy to talk about. Not to mention I've been a little busy. I was doing all those pesky things like kicking Patrick out, finding a lawyer, and convincing my mom that I did not need to move in with her." I clicked my seat belt into place, tightening it.

"By the time I had a moment's peace, this trip was only a few weeks away. Girls' Trip is for drinking and debauchery, not divorce talk."

"Well, you found the time to tell me."

I snorted. "No, I didn't. You just happened to be on the phone with me when I walked in and caught the man I've been married to for the last five years nailing his brand-new secretary."

I side-eyed the guy who'd sneezed relatively close to my shoulder.

"You found out by default." I looked over at one of my favorite people in the world. Kasey and I met in college at a party our freshman year. We bonded over our love of oldies music and ice-cold beer. Right now, her big brown eyes were full of love and support. I knew she was right, but I was in no way, shape, or form about to ruin our yearly girls' trip with my soon-to-be divorce. "Please drop it for now, Kasey. I *need* this weekend, and I need it to be drama free."

My three best friends and I took one trip a year together, *one*. I wasn't about to spend the next three days doing anything other than drinking, dancing, and laughing with my tribe.

"I'm about to take my antianxiety drops so I can make it through this damn flight." I held up the little brown dropper bottle in my hands. "I swear I miss the old days when we were broke college kids and couldn't afford to fly anywhere." I put two drops of the holistic calming meds under my tongue, ignoring Kasey's laughter. She knew I hated to fly, they all knew I hated to fly. But here I was, yet again, on another flight.

Kasey gasped beside me, then started to shake my shoulder. "Livi, look, is that our pilot? I swear I saw that guy at the bar this morning when we were drinking breakfast."

"Stop. It." I narrowed my eyes trying to determine if she was kidding.

"I'm serious." She was smiling though, fighting back laughter, so she had to be joking.

"Serious pain in my ass. Now leave me alone. You aren't funny." I closed my eyes and tried to steady my breathing. Within a few minutes I started to feel a little woozy, like I'd drunk half a bottle of wine. Hmmm this was a nice way to fly. Within another sixty seconds I felt like I'd switched from wine to tequila. These holistic people knew their stuff.

"Livi? Livi."

I opened one eye when I heard my name. "What now? Did you see our flight attendant doing lines in the bathroom?"

"What? No. We landed. We're here."

I opened the other eye, looking past her out the little round window, amazed that we were on the tarmac. "Really? I slept through the whole flight? I'm gonna be pissed if we haven't even taken off yet, Kasey, I swear—"

"We're really here, weirdo. You've been asleep for like three hours." She started digging around in her purse, grabbing her phone and turning it on. "You're terrible company."

I sat up straighter, stretching my arms above my head. "Sorry. Either I was tired or those are some badass holistic meds my yoga instructor gave me." I felt so alive and refreshed, I needed to send her limber ass a thank you note.

We waited until it was our turn to get off the plane, which seemed to take an eternity. When we rounded the corner, following the signs to baggage claim, I stopped short and put my arm out to get Kasey's attention. "Uh, why is there a handsome young man holding a sign with our names on it? Are we being *Punk'd*?" I started looking around, checking for a hidden camera crew or Ashton Kutcher.

"*Punk'd*?"

The sign holder was more than handsome, he was like handsome times infinity. He had this studious-boy-next-door thing going on. Short blond hair and kind green eyes that were darting all around the airport, searching for us apparently.

Kasey snorted. "What is this, two thousand and three? No one gets *Punk'd* anymore." She tilted her head, giving him an appreciative once-over. "Bailey probably hired drivers so we wouldn't have too many cars at the lake house. Let's head to baggage claim, our luggage should be there by now."

Kasey walked off to grab our bags, I didn't follow her; she was stronger than me. She was used to carrying a toddler on her hip all day, she could handle our two suitcases. Instead, I went to talk to tall, blond, and handsome with the sign. I was too intrigued to wait, and he was clearly looking for us.

"Excuse me, um, sir? I'm Livi. Of Livi and Kasey." I pointed to his sign. "As appealing as this all, uh, seems, did someone send you for us? Because neither Kasey nor Livi," I pointed to the sign again, "would have had the foresight to hire a car service."

He dropped said sign down by his side, giving me an easy smile. "Your friend Bailey hired us." He reached out and took the carry-on strap that was resting on my shoulder.

"Us?" I smiled back. I had no choice, his voice had an adorable Southern edge to it, and was making me slightly giddy. Either that or my meds hadn't worn off completely.

"Yes, ma'am." There it was again, that melt-your-panties-off Southern drawl. "Bailey hired two of us for the weekend. We're from Club Concierge." When all he got in response was silence and my mouth hanging open, he chuckled. "Your friend basically hired male butlers for the next three days."

My eyes went wide. "Oh."

Every girls' trip we joked about hiring some hot man-candy to wait on us hand and foot. And every year we never actually went through with it. Bailey liked to spoil her friends, but hot-man butlers? That took the cake. I glanced behind me as Kasey struggled her way over to join us. The buff butler man handed me the sign and went to help her. Well, he certainly seemed good at his job, didn't he?

"Who did *what*? What did I miss while I was wrestling *all* of our luggage?" Kasey blew her chocolate brown bangs out of her face and shot me a dirty look. "Thanks for the help by the way."

My eyes darted to our new friend. He'd gotten on his cell phone, but I whispered all the same. "Bailey hired us hot-man butlers for the weekend."

"Shut. Up."

"I will not." I pursed my lips, gesturing with my head to the cutie with my carry-on. "That's what *Southern charm* over there said. Apparently, she hired two of them." Please God let the other one be as gorgeous and as Southern as the one easily holding all our bags in his muscular arms. Not that Southern men were in short supply where we were from, we lived in Texas, but let me tell you, there is a difference between the South and the Deep South. FYI, the Deep South, was my weakness. That's not really a pun intended type thing, although it could be. You ladies know what I'm talking about.

When butler number one got off his phone, Kasey stuck out her hand in greeting. "I'm Kasey. It's nice to meet you."

He shifted my bag to his other arm so he could shake her hand. "Cole. Nice to meet you." He glanced to me. "Both of you." He gestured in front of him, indicating that we should go ahead. "My buddy is pulling the truck around to pick us up."

If his buddy was even half as adorable as Cole, it was going to be a hell of a weekend.

Chapter Two

Livi

When we finally made our way out of the crowded airport and got to the curb, a big black Suburban drove up. The back hatch opened automatically and cool air whooshed out. It was hot and humid as hell outside; the AC leaking from the truck was more than welcome.

Cole loaded our bags inside and then opened the back door for us and we climbed in, me first, then Kasey. After our adorable new friend Cole got into the passenger seat and shut the door, the SUV pulled away from the airport terminal. Between the window tinting and the overhang blocking the sunlight, it was extremely dark in the car. I couldn't really see the person driving, and believe me, I was trying.

Real, real hard.

Cole turned in his seat to introduce us. "Kasey, Livi, this is Taylor. Taylor, Kasey and Livi."

"It's nice to meet you ladies. Are y'all excited for your girls' weekend?" Taylor's voice floated back to us and I melted into a puddle on the leather seat. Thank you lord for the two sweet blessings sitting in the front. I could look *and* touch. Not that I would, I was a little too old for weekend flings, and my divorce wasn't even final yet. But the point was, ladies, I *could*. So taken with his voice and the delicious thoughts free-wheeling in my head, I forgot he asked a question.

Luckily Kasey answered and saved me from looking like a total airhead. "Are you kidding? A whole weekend where the only person I need to be responsible for is myself? I look forward to this all year." Cole and Taylor both chuckled. I wondered if that was part of their job. Humoring the women, because like I said, Kasey wasn't that funny.

Eventually, we got out from under the overhang and the inside of the car brightened considerably. I was one hundred percent unprepared for what I saw when I glanced in the review mirror. Taylor was core-clenching hot. The kind of hot that hurts. He had the palest blue eyes I'd ever seen set in a face lightly kissed by Georgia summers. With dirty blond hair that was curling out from under a faded Georgia Bulldogs baseball cap that he wore backwards, he radiated country boy cool. From what I could see of his hands on the wheel, his arms were full of muscle and definition, not in a gross beefy way, but in an easy I-bale-hay-in-my-free-time kind of way.

My insides went up in flames, he was that gorgeous.

When I was able to tear my eyes away from his forearms to look back at his handsome face in the rearview mirror, he was staring right at me. He'd caught me checking him out, red freaking handed. I should have been embarrassed, but I wasn't. No ma'am. Instead of shying away, or trying to play it off, I held his gaze. He was the first one to break eye contact. Probably a good thing considering he was driving. I bet their Google rating would go way down if they killed us.

Taylor cleared his throat, projecting his voice to reach us in the backseat. "So, are all of y'all married?"

I answered quickly and without thinking. "Oh, I'm not married." Kasey jabbed me in the side. "Ouch." I turned to her, whispering, "What? I'm *not.*"

Kasey murmured back to me, "If you don't want our friends to know you're getting divorced, then maybe you shouldn't tell people that you aren't married." She shook her head and answered Taylor, "The rest of us are. Married, I mean. *Happily* married."

I wrinkled my nose. "He didn't ask you to fuck him Kasey, calm down." Then I sighed, knowing she was right about the other thing. "Uh, guys? I'm not married, honestly, I'm getting divorced. But I don't really want the other girls to know that yet. So, please forget I said anything. Okay?"

Cole quickly nodded his head. "No problem."

Taylor caught my eye in the rearview mirror, sexy smirk in place. "Oh, I won't forget. I won't say anything to your friends, but I certainly won't be forgetting."

I held his gaze a second time. When he broke away to look at the road, I leaned over and stage whispered to Kasey. "Is he hitting on me? It's been so long since someone hit on me, I can't tell."

"Yes, he is. And don't even think about it." Kasey gave me her most stern mom look. It never worked on her son Knox, and it wasn't going to work on me. She turned her attention back to the front seat. "So. How in the world did you two get into this line of work?"

Cole answered, "For most of us it's just a part-time gig. Something interesting to do to put ourselves through college. I'm a couple semesters away from graduating and heading to law school, and Taylor is graduating next month as well. It beats waiting tables or stripping, and the money is way better."

I asked, "Is it fun? I mean, working with women all the time? Are people ever super bossy and bitchy?"

"Nah. Ninety percent of the time it's women like you and your friends. Looking for a fun weekend and some laughs." Cole got his phone out again; I saw that he pulled up his maps app. "We should be arriving in about ten minutes."

Bailey found us this beautiful house on Lake Hartwell. It was supposed to be only a few miles from this quaint little tourist town in southern Georgia. All the pictures she sent us online made the place look so tranquil.

When we first started this yearly tradition, we would search out places to party. Sun, shots, and swinging from the chandeliers. Now, we looked for places off the beaten path to relax and recharge. Apparently, in this case, a place with enough room for two personal butlers.

Bailey was nonstop fun, and she was too rich for her own good. It didn't surprise me she hired men to be at our beck and call all weekend. We talked about it every year. How amazing it would be to have gorgeous men bring us drinks and drive us around. A fun time with hot men, without being hit on every two seconds, or getting into trouble with our husbands.

Huh, guess I didn't really have to worry about that now. Lucky me. And I meant that. I wasn't being sarcastic. My husband cheated on me. My marriage was over. I deserved to ogle hot dudes for three days.

I peeked over at Taylor's profile. Holy hell, he was extremely good-looking. I wondered what I looked like after a three-hour flight where I slept like the dead. Probably not so great.

Chapter Three

Taylor

Damn, she was beautiful. Honestly, Livi was one of the most beautiful women I'd ever seen. Since I'd taken this gig I could say, in my line of work, I'd seen my fair share. Old women, young women, flirty women, rich women, a lot of plastic women. There was something innocent about Livi though, something wholesome.

Which made me want to get her very, very dirty.

She had hair the color of honey and it fell down her back in these no-fuss waves. She had stunning, dark green eyes that tipped up on the ends, and her little button nose had a light dusting of freckles. Her skin was smooth and flawless, and her lips, my god, her lips. I wanted to suck on them until they were red and swollen.

Since I didn't want to be too obvious, I didn't turn around in my seat to check out her body. Thankfully, we were going to be at a lake for three days. I was sure I'd get a chance to see her in a bikini. *Or naked?* I'd shoot for seeing her naked. I mean, dream big, right?

To top it all off, she was the only girl on this trip not married.

It was like a summer miracle.

We weren't supposed to hit on the women we were working for, let alone bone them, but this was my last butler job *ever*. I was graduating with a degree in sociology in three weeks. Then it was off to the real world, the boring world, the world I wanted nothing to do with. I might as well have my fun while I still could.

I glanced in the rearview mirror again when I heard the sound of Livi laughing. It must have been something Cole said. It irritated me that he'd been the one to make her laugh that freely. Her head was thrown back and her neck looked so damn kissable.

I wanted to make her laugh like that. Why? I couldn't fucking tell ya.

"Tay, are you listening to me?"

"Huh? What?" I glanced over at Cole; he looked annoyed.

He shook his head and mumbled under his breath so only I could hear, "Stop thinking with your dick, man, she's not for you," then louder he said, "we take a right up there where that wooden sign is. You see it?"

"Yeah, man, I see it." I steered the glorified mommy mobile the company made us use onto the narrow driveway.

The house that stood before us was amazing. I'd been coming to this lake with my family since I was a little boy, but I'd never seen this place before. It was new construction, but built to look old. A lot of worn wood surrounded by decades-old trees. It had a screened-in front porch, balconies on the second story, and a spectacular view of the lake. Damn, I loved my life. I was getting paid to spend the whole weekend at a gorgeous house, flirting with a beautiful *not* married girl.

I put the car in park and everyone jumped out. Cole went around the car and grabbed a couple bags from the back, and then he and Kasey headed up the drive. I patiently waited for Livi to step beside me.

"So pretty."

Livi leaned in and grabbed a suitcase, dragging it out of the back and then almost toppled over from the weight of it. "Yeah, Bailey has really outdone herself this time. This view is incredible." She glanced over her shoulder, eyeing the glittering lake.

I traded her one of the smaller bags I was carrying for the larger one that she was bound to drop on her toe. Or mine.

When her gaze moved up to mine, I winked. "I wasn't talking about the house."

She rolled her eyes, a smile dancing on her pretty face. "Nice line, kid."

"*Kid*? I'm pretty sure we're about the same age." I bit my lip, women loved that. "And it wasn't a line. I think you're gorgeous. Spend the weekend in bed with me."

Totally forward, I knew that, but I found that taking big risks usually resulted in bigger rewards. Livi had been checking me out in the rearview on the drive over. She liked what she saw, and I could see the appreciation in her eyes. Plus, she'd all but shouted that she was single as soon as I'd asked.

She was interested. Whether she let herself act on it was the gamble.

"What?" Livi started laughing so hard that it took her a few minutes to compose herself and answer me. "Absolutely not."

Not a polite no, but *absolutely not*? Talk about a bruise to your ego. "Why?" I had never been turned down that quickly before. No joke. Never, ever.

"Let's see. Number one." She shot me a pointed look. "I literally *just* met you. Number two, I'm here on a girls' weekend. And number three, my friends still think I'm married. I'm pretty sure banging you in the next room would tip them off something was wrong since I'm not the cheating type." She started to walk up the purposefully worn wooden steps, calling over her shoulder. "Plus, isn't that like against company policy or something?"

I grabbed her free hand, pulling her back down a step to me. "I didn't hear anywhere in your numbered list of reasons that you didn't *want* to spend the weekend with me. FYI, this is my last job. I graduate in a few weeks so I don't care if they fire me."

She rolled her eyes again, took her hand out of mine, and walked the rest of the way up to the porch. She stepped inside and I could instantly hear her and her friends' high-pitched delight at seeing each other. *Girls.*

You know what I said to my friends when I hadn't seen them in a while? *Hey, man, what's up.*

I waited for all the squealing to stop before I entered the house, making sure I had a sexy smirk on my face. I needed that first impression to be a real gut punch, get the lusty thoughts going right away. "All right, ladies. Where do I need to put these bags?"

It was Bailey who answered me, she was the one we had been emailing back and forth to set this whole weekend up, and she was the only one not zeroed in on my straining forearms. Man, I loved girls' weekends.

"Well, I was about to ask everyone how they wanted to do sleeping arrangements. There is one bedroom with a full-size bed, which I claimed for myself." She paused and gave everyone a glittery smile. "Another bedroom with a king and then a room with a bunk bed that the guys are using. So either all three of you can fit in the king or there is one other bed, it's a full but it's on the side porch. It's screened in and the owner promises me that the fan they have out there keeps it plenty cool at night."

My gaze immediately darted to Livi. I was mentally pleading with her to take the outside bed. If she took that bed, there was a damn good chance I could charm my way into it. It was secluded from her friends, and she'd be alone. I knew she wanted me, now I needed to convince her to act on it.

Livi raised her hand. "I'll take the outside bed. I don't mind."

Hell to the yes. I fought the urge to drop to my knees so I could properly thank the powers that be for my good fortune.

Kasey spun and narrowed her eyes on me. Crap, did I fist pump for real or only in my head?

One of the other girls, whose name I couldn't remember, asked Livi if she was sure about the outside room. Livi nodded, smiling. "Really, I don't mind at all. Maybe I'll be able to get a little work done in the mornings too."

Other girl, whose name I really should learn, pointed at Livi. "No ma'am. No work this weekend." Then she turned, eyeing Cole and me. "Although the scenery here is pretty inspiring."

Were we scenery? I gave a mental shrug. Whatever. It wasn't the first time a girl had called me inspiring. Other girl was platinum blonde, leggy, and sassy.

I took Livi's bags out onto the side porch, wearing an enormous smile, and placed them under the bed. I took a quick look around, checking out the space. The room was perfect. The bed was made with lightweight white linens, the antique iron frame wasn't against any restrictive walls. Plenty of room to work.

There was a door that led to the outside, I could easily slip in and out without being seen by anyone in the house. Plus, with that high-powered fan in the corner, no one would be able to hear her screaming my name.

Chapter Four

Livi

I saw Taylor's face when the option of the lone bed came up. I saw the look in his eyes. *Hope*. And what did I do? I encouraged it. Not too smart, Livi, you cannot have a weekend-long sex-fest with that man. You cannot. You are almost thirty, not twenty. Pull yourself together, woman.

Although. I *was* getting divorced, and didn't most people going through a breakup need a rebound? Taylor was so pretty, and his voice, holy hell his voice. I could listen to that man read me the damn dictionary.

I jumped when my friend Allie touched my arm. "Liv, you okay? You went blank there for a minute?"

"Yeah, no, never better. What's the game plan, Allie cat? Drinks?" I nodded once and then looped my arm through hers, dragging her to the kitchen. I needed a distraction, and I needed Allie to stop noticing my blank stares into fantasy land. "We could use a drink."

Allie laughed, shaking her head. "No ma'am. Bailey hired the cuties specifically for that reason."

"Nooooo," I wailed dramatically. "Will you please make it? Pretty please with cherries on top? You've been making my drinks for twelve years. You know how I like them. Hotties one and two don't." I clasped my hands in front of me, pleading for a perfectly made vodka drink.

"Ugh. Fine." She pointed an impeccably manicured finger in my direction. "Look, I'll show them how to do it, and then the rest of the weekend I'm off bartender duty. Deal?"

"Deal." I slapped her ass as she walked away. Allie worked her way through her degree behind the bar at one of our favorite college hangouts. You know that one friend who can talk you into anything? Everyone has one. Well, Allie was mine.

Hey, Livi, let's drive across two states and spend the weekend with these guys I just met. Okay.

Hey, Livi, we're going to sleep in this horse trailer tonight so we don't have to drive home. Sure.

Hey, Livi, mixed drinks in the beer bong is the same thing as beer in the beer bong.

Sounds good.

Those exact conversations actually took place.

Bailey joined Allie at the bar, and once everyone had a drink in hand she proposed a toast. "Here's to girls' weekend. So hard."

I raised my drink and we all repeated after her. "So hard."

It was tradition, this was girls' trip number eleven. Our first one had been a quick weekend getaway to the Texas Gulf Coast, where the water is brown and the sand is littered with sharp shells and dead fish.

I took a big gulp. I coughed as the burn hit the back of my throat and then shot daggers across the bar at Allie; little brat added a surprise floater on the top of my cocktail. Taylor patted my back a few times. When I didn't stop him, he started to rub his palm in big sweeping circles, then his hand dropped dangerously close to my ass. Since clearly I wasn't choking for real, and clearly he *was* trying to put the moves on me, I stepped away from his touch.

I moved closer to Bailey who, not surprisingly, was still talking "So as you all can see, we have two handsome men with us on this trip. They are here to do the heavy lifting. Bartend, drive us around, take us on hikes, dance with us, make us laugh…all that fun stuff. They are nice guys. Be nice to them." She pointed out into the crowd. "Allie, I'm talking to you."

Allie put her hand to her chest in mock indignation. "Me? Well I never."

Bailey was right to call her out. Allie had a bit of a bitchy streak. Luckily her fun-loving streak was much wider.

"We want to thank y'all for having us." Cole smiled, he could be a politician with his adorable grin, baby face, and sa-weet Southern accent. "This place is stunning and you all are beautiful, this hardly feels like work. If there is anything y'all need, please don't hesitate to ask, that's what we're here for."

I shivered when Taylor stepped up behind me and whispered in my ear. "Day or night, sugar."

I turned to face him with every intention of telling him it wasn't going to happen. But damn, the man standing behind me was so freaking gorgeous. I was rendered speechless and it took me a full thirty seconds to recover and find my grown-up voice.

"Do you ever give up?"

He winked as he sauntered away.

Oh yeah, he was going to be calling my bluff at some point tonight. The only question was, what would my answer be? Taylor had trouble written all over his perfectly sculpted tan body and I could already feel my thin resolve crumbling.

The kitchen cleared as we all went to change into our swimsuits. Not only was the house right on the lake, but it also had a huge in-ground pool. I stepped out onto my porch/bedroom that was completely screened in and had a great view of the woods and the water.

Everything was so green and lush. The lake was practically sparkling like someone had sprinkled glitter on top, and I wondered how many people had run down the planked dock and jumped in. How many kids had screamed with delight as they flew off the edge into the cool water?

I turned my attention to the room itself. It had an antique bed, a small wooden nightstand, and a huge box fan, and that was it. Although, with the panoramic views, the little space didn't need anything else to make it feel magical.

When I crouched down to look under the bed for my bags, I was confused. There were three bags under there and I only brought two. I pulled the foreign duffle out and unzipped it. Resting on top was a Georgia Bulldogs tank top, size L. I shook my head. *Really?* Did Taylor really put his things under my bed? I could act offended, even though I really wasn't, or I could have a little fun with the adorably relentless guy who wanted in my panties.

I changed into my bikini and then put on Taylor's tank top. It came to mid-thigh and the arm holes were so big you could see right through one to the other side. As I strolled out onto the pool deck, Cole choked on the water he was drinking. I tried my best not to laugh and ruin the moment along with my cool swagger. When I glanced over at Taylor, I saw his eyes travel up and down my body. He bit his lower lip, like he was trying to hide his grin.

"Nice shirt."

I smiled at him over my shoulder as I walked past. "Thanks."

Chapter Five

Taylor

I have never seen anything sexier than Livi wearing my shirt. Holy fuck. What was it about that girl that had me all tangled up? This wasn't me. I could get who I wanted, when I wanted. She was ballsy though, I'd give her that, coming out in my clothes. Almost as ballsy as I'd been sliding my duffle under her bed.

"Is it yours?" I narrowed my eyes, studying the hem of my shirt and the way it kissed the top of her thighs as she sauntered away.

Livi pursed her perfect lips and shrugged one shoulder. "It was in my room right along with all my other stuff, so I guess it is now."

I crossed my arms over my chest and leaned against the porch railing. "I didn't know you were a Bulldogs fan."

She smiled, coyly, over her shoulder. "You met me an hour ago, Taylor. There's lots of things about me you don't know."

I watched as she wandered down to the pool, sipping from her cup along the way. My whole body was pushing me to follow her, and once I reached her, throw her over my shoulder and drag her off caveman style.

Bailey came out the door, blocking my fantastic view of Livi's retreating ass. "Hey, y'all come on down and swim with us. Make a drink, have some fun. We aren't doing any driving tonight, and I promise not to tell."

Hell, she didn't need to ask me twice. I stepped over to the cooler and pulled out two cans. I popped the tops off the ice-cold beers and handed one to Cole. I didn't wait on him before I went to join the girls. Their laughter was inviting, and Livi was like a homing beacon for my cock.

I sat down on the edge of the pool, dangling my feet in the tepid water. Georgia was already sweltering. The pool didn't stand a chance of staying cool. "So, you all know each other exceptionally well I gather." I gestured to Cole with my beer as he made his way down to us. "But we know nothing about any of you. What do y'all do outside of vacationing without your husbands?"

Allie went first. I'd finally heard someone else refer to her by her name. "I'm in oil."

Bailey held her hand up. "Acquisitions."

Kasey answered, "Real estate."

Ah, the best for last, Livi. I leaned forward, not wanting to miss a word she said. "I, uh, I work from home. I'm a writer."

"Tell him what you write, Livi," Allie prompted with a wicked smile on her face. "We're sharing here." Livi shot a death glare at her friend. But before Livi could answer for herself, Allie answered for her. "Porn."

Cole spewed beer out of his mouth. Man, he was having the worst luck with liquids around these chicks. First the water he'd choked on when he spotted Livi in my shirt and now the beer. I was proud of myself, I didn't even bat an eye at Allie's declaration. Don't get me wrong, inside I was jumping up and down like a fucking cheerleader, but outside, I was stoic. Totally cool.

"So, porn. Like romance novels, mom porn stuff, or like you write the scripts for actual pornos?"

Livi took a sip of her cocktail, then set her cup on the concrete by my thigh. "Romance novels, not porn scripts."

"Interesting." I gave her my most charming smile. "If you need any new material, any inspiration, let me know. I'd be *more* than happy to help."

She raised a flawlessly shaped eyebrow. "Oh yeah? You think you got lines I haven't heard before, kid?"

WTF. Again with the kid. I couldn't let that stand. "Sugar, one weekend with me, and you'll be able to write ten new books." I winked for added effect.

Livi held my stare, smirking. I could tell she didn't want to look away, and neither did I. I would spend the next eight hours locked in a staring match if it meant her attention was on me that long. I was like a fucking puppy, jumping at her ankles, begging to be picked up.

Then fucking Bailey, the bossy one, ruined our moment by loudly clearing her throat. "Uh, Liv, don't you think Patrick would have a problem with that?"

Livi's forehead wrinkled in confusion. She looked adorable when she was confused. "Who?"

Bailey narrowed her eyes. "Patrick. Your husband."

"Aww, crap. I'm married."

I couldn't help but chuckle at Livi's response, although Bailey appeared downright mortified. Livi nodded emphatically. "Yes. You are correct. Patrick most likely would not like that." Livi was still smiling though, and I took that as a good sign.

Cole asked, "Do y'all have kids?"

And I totally tuned out of the conversation when Livi pulled *my* shirt over her head, threw it on the chair behind her. It was the moment I'd been looking forward to since I caught her checking me out in the car ride here. Livi in a bikini.

As if her face, hair, smile, and laugh weren't enough to make a guy fall to his knees and beg her to notice him, that banging body had my name written all over it. I wasn't letting her get farther than three feet away from me.

Vaguely, I heard that Kasey say she had a son, but everyone else was childless. I couldn't care less. No way could I tear my gaze away from Livi. Her eyes had gone blank and her lips into a tight smile when Cole had mentioned kids. Almost like shutting down was a practiced response.

Suddenly, I wanted to pull her aside and ask her a thousand questions about her life. I wanted to know everything about her. Why? I couldn't say.

Chapter Six

Livi

Talking about kids made my heart hurt a little. It always did. I had practically been begging Patrick to have a baby for two years now. He always had some excuse. Work was crazy, he was traveling too much, he wanted to buy a bigger house. It was all bullshit. He didn't want to have kids. When we first started dating, we talked about children, and he had seemed so excited about the idea of being a dad. Over time, his wants and needs changed.

He became money hungry and so driven that it'd become a fault. Then he cheated. Who knows? Maybe his wants and needs changed because he'd been cheating all along. I mean, that secretary was brand new and he had her sprawled out over his desk like they'd been fucking for years. Either he'd installed her outside his office, or, more likely, he banged whoever he could get to spread her legs. Being married didn't factor for him.

Patrick kept begging me to forgive him, like down on his knees begging. Maybe if it'd been a one-off, I might've forgiven him, but knowing the hours he kept and the excuses he'd made over the years, blondie was probably the most recent in a long line of many. Even so, the cheating wasn't why I was divorcing him. It was simply the final nail in the coffin of everything that was wrong with us.

I took a big gulp of my still-way-too-strong drink and plastered a smile on my face. I looked up and caught Taylor studying me, his eyes full of mischief. He was making me tingle in places that had no right to be tingling.

"So, Livi, porn?"

I nodded. "Well, the polite term is erotic romance." I rarely ever told strangers that I wrote romance novels for a living. The questions were often inappropriate and unintelligent.

"How in the hell did you decide to write erotic romance novels? I mean when I picture a romance writer, I picture an older lady, lots of cats, no dates..."

"That's extremely narrow-minded and stereotypical, but somewhat comical, so I'll let it slide." I shrugged, wading through the water, moving closer to him. "It's not like I woke up one day and thought, *hey I feel like writing love scenes*. It just sort of happened. But it's fun and I get paid to do it. No pun intended." If I knew how to wink, I would've winked at him. I had to settle for a flirty smile instead. "What about you? What do you do when you aren't trying to bed rich divorcees?"

"First of all, I don't ever try to *bed* our clients." He leaned forward so far he was practically touching the water with his chest before he whispered, "You're special." Then he stood up. "Like I said earlier, I'm a few weeks away from graduating. I'll have a degree in sociology, which I'll waste working for my father. I don't need this job after Sunday."

I nodded, all the pieces falling into place. Taylor's cocky sex appeal, his confidence. "Correct me if I'm wrong here, but spoiled rich kid, daddy owns half the town, side job and degree are both to piss him off, which is futile because, for some reason or another, he still has you by the balls. Eventually, you will fall in line: trophy wife, two point five kids, and a yellow lab."

Taylor took a deep breath, cocking his head to the side. "That's extremely narrow-minded, stereotypical, but somewhat comical, so I'll let it slide." He slipped into the water, sinking all the way under before popping back up and shaking his hair out of his perfect face.

Allie floated over to us on her back, slowly peddling through the water with her hands. "Whatever y'all are talking about, it sounds boring." She flipped over and stood next to me, peering into my cup. "You should drink faster."

I put my hand on her forehead, pushing her face away from my cup. "You made my drink a double, you ass. I have to take my time or I'll be asleep in an hour."

Taylor smiled against his beer bottle. "Is Livi prone to passing out?"

Allie laughed, splashing water in my direction. "Oh yeah, she used to be for sure. One time, when we were in college, Kasey, Livi, and I closed down the bars, but there was a party that Kasey and I wanted to hit. We put Liv in the backseat and before we even got the car started she was curled up in a ball, asleep. We locked her ass in there and partied without her. She never even knew."

Taylor pressed his beautiful lips together, making them a thin line. "She doesn't still do that, does she? Would be such a shame to waste a perfectly good night, sleeping."

I cut my eyes from Allie to Taylor, his gaze was once again dark and steely. I caught the innuendo and wondered if Allie did too. Not that she would give me a hard time about it. Out of all my friends Allie was the least judge-y.

I shook my head, playing along for no other reason than that I could. "Nah, I can go all night long now." I hid my smile in my cup.

I was playing with fire, and I'd been doing it since I'd laid eyes on this Taylor character. I wasn't sure why I was flirting with him or what my end game was, but I seemed to really enjoy getting a rise out of him. Pun *not* intended.

Chapter Seven

Taylor

I can go all night long now... Livi's hot little body in that tiny black bikini, coupled with her sexy innuendo...she'd given me a semi. If I played my cards right, I had a feeling this could be an unforgettable weekend. Cole and I left the girls down by the pool to start dinner. By left I mean he had to drag me reluctantly back to the house and demand I do my actual job.

We were grilling steaks for them. Not too difficult: throw some meat and potatoes on the fire. Standing with Cole by the grill, beer in hand, watching Livi laugh with her friends by the water. It all felt domestic and cozy for some reason. Odd because I had never felt domestic in my entire life. Not at home with my two workaholic parents, and certainly not in response to some chick I was into.

I closed my eyes and took another pull off my beer. I needed to remember who I was. I was Taylor Hill. I was a fucking legend. I played baseball for four years at the University of Georgia. I *bagged more tail than team Real Tree*. I put myself through school flirting with women. Well, my parents put me through school, but my fun little job paid my often enormous bar tab.

Either way you sliced it, I was a badass.

"Hey, badass, could you hand me the butter?"

I opened my eyes. Did I call myself a badass out loud? Not particularly badass of me. "Yeah, here you go, man."

Cole used the butter to coat the grill before putting the steaks on. Then he sat down in one of the overly padded chairs on the patio and trained his eyes on me. "What are you doing, Tay?"

I sat in the chair opposite his, turning it slightly so I could still see Livi. I was becoming a bit of a creep. "Giving myself a mental pep talk. What are you doing, C?"

"Wondering what the hell your end game is blatantly hitting on a married chick."

Hmm, Cole's self-righteousness was showing.

I looked around to make sure all the girls were still by the water. "Dude, you know Livi's getting divorced."

He rolled his eyes. "It's not even final yet, man."

"So? I'm not asking to be her new husband. I'm asking Livi to have some fun with me for three days."

Both of us looked out at the pool. Livi was grinding on Bailey to some seriously old-school rap and cracking up about it. She looked carefree and fun. Edible. When I brought my gaze back to Cole, I noticed his were still on Livi. I snapped my fingers in front of his face. "Hey. Eyes over here. I hit on her first. Plus, you need a job for the next year or so. You can't get fired."

Cole shook his head, like an exasperated father. I should know, my own dad was constantly frustrated with me. "You need to leave her alone, Tay. She's here to have some fun with her friends. She's obviously going through something, and the last thing she needs is a weekend fling that she'll regret the moment her plane lands back in Texas."

I tore my eyes away from Livi to look at my *ex*-friend Cole. "First of all, no woman has *ever* regretted a fling with me. Second, I'm exactly what she needs right now. She needs to have some fun, feel desired, let go." I drained my beer. "We're both adults. What's the harm?"

Cole wrinkled his forehead, confused. "What's the harm? Well let's see, it could out her divorce to her friends, or even worse, they could think she's being unfaithful to her husband. Or she could fall for you and get all clingy. Which we both know how well you would deal with that. You could knock her up. I mean the list goes on and on."

I crossed my fingers on both hands and spit on the ground. "You bite your tongue, bro. If I knock her up, it's on you."

"Uh, no, that's not really how that—"

"I am smooth as glass. Her friends will never even know. As for her being a clinger? She doesn't really seem like the type."

Cole chuckled. "Jesus, Tay, you've known her for mere hours. How do you know what type of chick she is?"

I scoffed. "Women. It's what I do. And don't even act like I'm not a pro."

Cole crossed his arms over his chest. "I'm going to laugh my ass off when she ends up playing you. Leading you on, and then slamming the door in your face."

"Not gonna happen, C."

Should I tell him I already put my stuff in her room? Should I tell him it was already a done deal in my mind? That I *had* to have her this weekend? It was my new life goal and I would not fail? That the first time our eyes met my heart skipped a beat? That she could give me a semi with only a few words?

Nah. I should probably keep all that to myself.

Chapter Eight

Livi

Dinner was delicious. I couldn't remember the last time someone had cooked for me. Patrick was always working late, wait, scratch that. Patrick was always out late screwing women who weren't his wife. It'd been so ingrained in me to throw out excuses for why he was absent from dinner parties and nights with our friends. *He's working.* I'd said it so many damn times, over and over. How many of those times had I been lying because I'd been lied to? I didn't miss him, and I knew that spoke volumes about the state our marriage had reached before the crashing end.

I sighed, polishing off the drink in my hand. This weekend wasn't about Patrick, it was about my and friends and I. Rehashing the past wasn't going to help anyone right now.

We all sat together at a long dining table and ate, drank, and laughed until we couldn't move. I was for sure buzzed. Kasey and Bailey were flat out wasted. They were dancing on their chairs and singing at the top of their lungs. Salt-N-Pepa always brought out their crazy. Allie and I were standing at the bar pouring a round of shots.

Cole came over and leaned on the bar across from us, eyebrows raised in question. "Shots?"

"Shots," I answered with a smile.

Cole turned, watching Bailey and Kasey dance for a few moments. "You think those two need any more alcohol?"

Allie snorted. "Oh son, this isn't our first rodeo. Those two get the super special shot glasses, where the vodka is actually water."

I handed two bomb cups to Cole. "These are for them. Please." I laughed as I watched him mosey up to the table to deliver the drinks. Bailey took one and handed Kasey hers and then they pulled Cole up on the table with them and instructed him to dance. He shook his head but complied because these guys were nothing if not good sports. Allie handed one to me and passed one to Tay.

All the girls toasted, "So hard."

Cole spoke up above the music. "So what's the deal with the *so hard* toasts?"

Bailey pointed at me across the room and then beckoned me to the table with her finger. "Come on, Livi Lou, let's explain *so hard* to these boys."

I let out a playfully irritated breath but did as I was told. If I didn't, she would end up coming down and dragging me up there with her. It was always easiest to do what Bailey asked the first time.

I climbed up onto the table as Cole and Kasey climbed down, apparently giving Bailey and me the stage. With her curvy figure and long dark hair she was born to be in charge, to command a room.

She put her arms around my neck and kissed my cheek loudly. "Once upon a time we were down at the coast. It was our first girls' trip and we were all dragging. We had plans to go out that night, but two days of drinking had made us all so very weak." She made a pouty face before continuing, "Livi managed to rally first, which, let me tell you, was rare. She was dancing around, loading up the shot ski, jumping on beds…doing everything in her power to get us going again. Finally, she got me up and dressed and she and I were dancing in the kitchen."

I gave Bailey a wide smile. "She looked at me with this oddly serious look on her face and she said, *I'm going to dance on you so hard tonight.* I couldn't stop laughing. None of us could. It was the phrase of the night and we've toasted to that rally ever since."

Bailey had the remote to the speaker in her hand and after she was done with her tale of parties past, she turned the music back up. "Livi, will you please dance on me? So hard?"

Which I did. I danced on her embarrassingly hard. It was fun. It was out of control, but it was so much fun.

When the song ended, Taylor held his hand up to help me down. "I like to watch you with your friends. You look so carefree. They make you happy, don't they?"

My feet were on the ground but he hadn't let go of my hand. "They make me obscenely happy." I shrugged. "We've all been through so much together: broken hearts, first jobs, losing loved ones. The highest highs, and the lowest lows. I don't know what I would do without them." I squeezed his hand and then pulled mine away.

Taylor put his in his front pockets, pulling his shorts lower and drawing my eye to a newly exposed strip of tanned taut skin. "Then why don't you tell them what's going on?"

I gave him a sad smile, while trying to keep my eyes on his face and not his hips. "Because this whole weekend would turn into a pity party. They'd be worried about how I was feeling or how I was doing nonstop. They'd watch me like a hawk and it'd all be a giant buzzkill."

Taylor cocked his head, a wicked grin on his face. "Yeah, on second thought, don't tell them yet. I would hate to have an audience for what I plan on doing to you."

I couldn't help but chuckle at his unwavering confidence. "Smooth. Tell me again how many sad divorcées you've charmed into bed?" I crossed my arms over my chest, trying to go for mildly offended.

"None."

I snorted. "Liar."

"Why would I lie? I have never slept with a client. BTW, you are the farthest thing from a sad divorcée I have ever seen. What are you, like twenty-seven, twenty-eight? You're gorgeous and vibrant. I'm enamored."

My eyes got big. "You're *enamored*?"

Taylor looked down and rubbed the back of his neck like he was slightly embarrassed. "Yeah, sorry, I have no idea where that came from. I don't think I've ever used that word before, but for you, it fits."

The longer I was around him, the more he drew me in. If I were smart, I'd walk away. But instead, I stepped closer. "I'm thirty. How old are you?"

"Twenty-eight."

I let out a little laugh. "Wait, you're twenty-eight and just now graduating? Too much partying, not enough studying?"

"No. I played baseball my first four years at school, I took cake classes so I could keep my grades up. After I was done playing ball, I started taking classes for my major."

I pulled my lower lip through my teeth, because that was actually pretty smart, and smart was attractive. "Well. Either way, I'm older and wiser. Trust me when I say you're wasting your time trying to get me naked."

He threw his head back and laughed. "Oh sugar, there is nothing about you that could ever be a waste of my time. I'm not going to stop. You need me, and I want you. We're the perfect combination."

"I'm thirty, Taylor, not twenty. This isn't spring break my sophomore year of college. I'm not going to hop into bed with a guy because he's hot and he flirts with me."

"So you were easy in college?" He patted my shoulder, like he was comforting me. "It's okay. I was too."

"Wait. Crap. That's not what I meant."

He laughed again. I was starting to really love his laugh. It was so uninhibited and genuine. "I'm kidding, sugar. Look, I hear what you're saying. But try to have some fun with me, okay? When it stops being fun, tell me and I'll back off. Deal?"

I studied him before I answered. His blue eyes were bright and full of mischief, yet again. His smile was sexy. The way his chest looked in his t-shirt was sinful.

Yeah, I was an adult, but I wasn't dead. I wanted to have fun. Hell, after everything I'd been through, I deserved to have fun. I'd tried half-heartedly telling him no, but we'd both known I hadn't meant it. So really, what was the point in pretending he didn't turn me on? What was the point in denying myself some much needed...distraction?

I'd told Kasey that girls' trips were for drinking and debauchery. I'd had a few drinks, now maybe I should try out the debauchery.

"Deal."

Chapter Nine

Taylor

I had won a small victory with Livi, and I rode the high from it all the way into my next battle. Everyone had decided to call it a night, Livi was inside the house in the bathroom getting ready for bed. I was *in* her bed praying she wouldn't kick me out when she discovered me here. I was under the covers, wearing only my boxers. Presumptuous? Probably. Yet, I made sure my tanned chest was exposed, you know, to lure her in. I was wearing my reading glasses, thick black rims. I figured since she was a writer, she probably dug a guy in hipster glasses. I wasn't a poser though; I really did need them to read. I heard the screen door squeak open and I braced myself for her reaction.

She stopped short when she saw me, her eyes darting around the room. Almost like she was afraid someone was listening. "Taylor. What are you doing?"

"Studying." I looked down at the flash cards in my hand, ignoring her and reading to prove my point.

She took a few steps closer to me. "Why are you in my bed?"

"I like to think of it as *our* bed, sugar." I glanced up and gave her my most charming smile. The same smile that helped me get not one, not two, but *three* Kappa Sigs in the hot tub after homecoming junior year. I told you, I was a fucking legend.

She crossed her arms over her chest. Making her breasts look amazing in the relaxed gray tank top she was wearing. "Tay, this bed is the size of a postage stamp. There isn't enough room for both of us in here." Her words were saying no, but her bare legs were steadily bringing her closer.

"Still not hearing that you don't *want* me in your bed, sugar. Come hang out with me for a little while, and if you want me to leave, then I will." I held up the covers for her.

She stood there for a few moments, chewing her lip and apparently overthinking her next move. In the end, she rolled her eyes but climbed in.

Another victory.

She lay on her side facing me and picked up the papers on my lap. My dick jumped at how close her hand was. "What are these?" I shifted in bed, trying to keep a tenting situation from arising. Get it? *Arising*?

"Flash cards. It's the only way I've ever been able to study." I handed her a few. "Here, quiz me."

"Tay, its two o'clock in the morning, I don't want to study."

I fanned her face with my cards, making her hair blow back slightly. "Please, it'll really help me out."

"Fine," she snapped.

She took the glasses off my face and put them on hers. Holy hell she looked like every teacher fantasy I had ever had. The tenting was inevitable.

"Which concept seeks a consensus of opinion or group conformity by taking a narrow view of the issue?"

"Groupthink."

Livi turned the card over. "Very good." She pulled another one from my pile. "The social cohesion that results from the various parts of a society functioning as an integrated whole is?"

"Organic solidarity."

"Right again." She handed me back my glasses, signaling she was done. Livi closed her eyes and snuggled against my body, her forehead touching the side of my shoulder. Even the small gesture of her forehead touching my skin was turning me on.

She sighed sleepily. "You smell good."

I smiled as I looked down at her pretty face. "Thank you, sugar." I stroked a finger across her cheek as lightly as I could. "So, you wanna make out?"

She grinned without opening her eyes. "Sure, but turn off the lamp and turn on the fan."

Holy shit. She said yes. I totally thought she was going to turn me down. I scrambled out of bed, tripping over my discarded pants, and did as I was told. When I climbed back in beside her, I lay down on my side, putting my face right next to hers. "I'm going to kiss you now."

She opened her eyes, they were so green, so beautiful. "Well, okay."

I closed the inches of space between us and lightly touched my lips to hers. They were so soft. I did it again, this time gently running my tongue along her bottom lip. I kept my kisses light and sweet, not knowing exactly what she wanted from me—afraid to go for too much and risk scaring her away. When I pulled back, her eyes were open once again and she was sporting an amused expression.

"Taylor, I'm not breakable."

"Thank god." I grabbed the back of her head and fused my mouth to hers. This time I didn't ask for permission, I slid my tongue into her mouth, swallowing her moan of approval.

She tasted like mint and perfection as she matched me stroke for stroke. I moved my hand from her head to her hip, pulling her pelvis to mine. I was impossibly hard for her and I wanted her to know it. Her free hand fisted in my hair, pulling slightly. We stayed like this, making out like teenagers, grinding our bodies together, our hands roaming all over each other.

She let me round first base, which was amazing. She had fake tits, but not like hard stone fake. Like awesome fake. This was fun, no doubt, but I wanted more. I wanted to taste every inch of her, I wanted to explore her body. I wanted to make her come so hard the fan wouldn't even drown out the sounds of her delight. When I tried to loosen the drawstring on her shorts, she stopped me.

"Taylor, I meant what I said earlier. I'm not going to have sex with someone I just met. It's irresponsible and slutty. I think once you hit thirty, slutty is sad."

I let out a deep breath; blue balls it was then. I'd told her multiple times that she was in the driver's seat, and I'd meant it. "Can I stay? Can we...spoon?"

I could see her disbelief in the moonlight. I couldn't blame her. I was having a hard time believing the words coming out of my mouth at the moment too. "Spoon, that's it? You aren't going to like jump on me the second I fall asleep, are you?"

"Tempting, but no. Just spoon. Promise."

She stared at me for a long time before she finally answered. "Fine. But you have to be gone as soon as the sun comes up."

I wanted to clap my hands at my third victory, but instead I remained calm and nodded. "I will be. Now roll over, I want to be the big spoon." She did what I asked.

Truth be told, I'd never been the big spoon before. I was always the one rolling away from whichever girl I was with. I'd let them spoon me until I was sure they were asleep and then I'd leave.

I never brought girls to my house, too risky for them to know where I lived. But here I was, wrapped around Livi like she was a damn life preserver. She felt so good in my arms, her little body fit against me like a glove. It was nicer than I thought it would be, holding her in my arms. Not like I was going to make a habit out of make-out sessions that ended in cuddles, but I could appreciate the appeal.

I buried my nose in her hair and fell asleep.

Chapter Ten

Livi

Thump, thump.

Thud.

Creak.

My eyes flew open at the sound of the screen door opening.

"Livi? Are you still asleep?" Allie was standing next to my bed, hands on her jogger-clad hips and her hair a chaotic mess around her face.

I sat up and looked down next to me, my heart pounding. No Taylor, thank god. "Uh, no. I'm awake. Just, uh, being lazy." When had he left? Had she seen anything? My eyes widened when I spotted Taylor's pants on the floor behind Allie. Holy shit. *Please don't turn around, please don't turn around.*

"Bailey made Bloody Marys, and Kasey made breakfast tacos. Come eat." I guess Allie was watching my eyes because she made a funny face and then started to turn around and follow my petrified gaze.

I yelled to get her attention, "Can I have a Michelada instead?" I reached out and grabbed her hand and clasped it in mine as I dragged her toward me. Like I was begging her to make me a drink. "Please-please-please."

Allie looked at me like I'd lost my mind. "Why are you yelling?"

"I, uh, I really want a Michelada. Please, Allie cat?"

She rolled her eyes but smiled. "Ugh. Fine. Spoiled brat."

I climbed out of bed, making sure to hold her gaze until she reached the door. "Love you."

"Yeah, yeah. Get dressed." She paused with her hand on the doorknob. "You never sleep the latest. You feeling okay?"

No. I'm not okay. I was up all night making out with a hot guy whose pants you literally stepped over two seconds ago. "Never better." I waited until I heard the screen door close before I collapsed back onto the bed and peered over the side about two feet away from the wall. Yep, there was Taylor, wedged under the bed, his face sticking out, his brows wiggling.

I couldn't help but giggle. "Quick thinking, kid. I thought you promised to be gone by the time the sun came up? Allie stepped all over your pants."

He pushed himself out a little and put his hands behind his head, appearing relaxed, which was impressive considering the tiny space his body was crammed into. "I did. But you felt so damn good all cuddled up next to me. I couldn't make myself leave."

"Such the smooth talker, even at eight a.m." I rested my cheek on the pillow he'd used. It still smelled like him. I had to fight the urge to take a deep inhale.

"Why were you screaming at her?"

"She was about to turn around and see your pants. I needed to distract her." I rolled over and got out of bed, tossing his pants behind me. "I'm going to go to the kitchen to keep distracting. You get up and leave through the side door." When I turned around to make sure he was being compliant, he was already gone.

I threw my hair into a messy bun on top of my head and went inside. Taylor walked in through the kitchen door at the same time I stepped into the living room. He caught my eye from across the room and winked.

Automatically, I smiled and Cole followed that smile back to Taylor and gave him the stink eye. "Tay man, where were you?"

Taylor didn't miss a beat. "I was hanging, looking at the lake. It's like glass out there today, so calm. So smooth. I haven't used any since I was a kid, but one of these hiking trails will take us to this awesome beachy area on the other side of the lake." He popped an olive into his mouth. "You girls game for some hiking?"

Bailey pulled a map out of a drawer in the kitchen and spread it open on the table. "I'm game. Come show me which trail."

Taylor chuckled. "We don't need a map, silly girl. I told you, I've been there before."

Kasey gave him a weary look. "You said you hadn't been since you were a kid. Do you honestly still remember how to get there?"

"Of course I do." He tapped the side of his head. "Steel trap."

Allie snorted. "Famous last words. We're all going to end up at a creepy abandoned cabin where we get chopped into pieces." As she leaned over the bar and handed me my drink, she asked, "Taylor, do you want a Bloody Mary?"

He shook his head. "Is there stuff left for another Michelada? I can make it myself. We're here to wait on you guys remember?"

I closed my eyes. Please don't let Allie realize what he'd let slip. *Please.* I cracked one eye to see Allie looking confused. "How did you know we had stuff for Micheladas?"

Taylor's eyes got big. He pursed his lips. "I, uh, can clearly...see the ingredients for Micheladas on the counter." He shook his head. "You girls are so fuzzy in the morning."

Allie looked down at the tomato juice, lime, and beer in front of her. "Oh, okay, duh."

Taylor sent me a relieved grin as he got busy making himself a drink and I got busy drinking mine.

I loved Allie, she was smart and successful, and had the world's best husband. But sometimes, she was naïve as hell.

When we were in college, she dated a drug dealer for like three months, and he was constantly getting into his own stash. To this day she swears he was independently wealthy and had ADHD.

Chapter Eleven

Taylor

I was off my game. Way fucking off. I had spent the whole night wrapped around Livi like a damn pansy. I never did that. I had almost outted our little sort of affair not once, but twice this morning. Then, twenty minutes into our hike I had been demoted to the back of the line. Apparently, my mind wasn't a steel trap after all. Bailey did not play around. The only positive thing going for me right now was that the back of the line gave me an amazing view of Livi's ass in her teeny tiny cutoff shorts.

After what seemed like a hundred miles, the thick woods gave way to the large open sandy lake entrance I remembered from my childhood. Totally grateful, we were the only ones here, and the water looked so welcoming. Everyone started peeling off their sweaty clothes so they could get in the water and cool off. I watched Livi shimmy out of her shorts and pull off her tank top. Red bikini today.

I knew I needed to keep my distance, but I couldn't seem to help myself where she was concerned. Instead of wading into the water with Cole, I walked up next to her and whispered close to her ear. "Come swim with me."

She put her hand to her face to shield her eyes from the sun as she studied the lake, her nose wrinkled. "Uh…no. I'll wade out into the water with you, knee deep, but I don't swim in lakes."

I made a face. "What? Why not?"

She didn't take her eyes off the water when she answered me. "Crocodiles, alligators, and/or piranhas."

I had to chuckle. "You're joking, right?"

Kasey laughed as she stepped past us. "Oh, she's serious. Liv watches way too many ridiculous scary movies. I'm surprised she slept on the porch by herself last night. I was sure I'd feel her crawling into bed with Allie and me at some point. You know, murderers in hockey masks and all that."

Livi groaned. "Dammit, Kasey, Jason hadn't even crossed my mind. Now it's going to be all I can think about tonight." Kasey rolled her eyes as she walked away.

I leaned down, placed my hand on Livi's hip, and let my lips brush her neck as I spoke. "Don't be silly, sugar. I'll be all you can think about tonight. I'll keep you safe." I picked her up, threw her over my shoulder, and headed into the water. I ignored her screams and threats. I didn't put her down until I was waist deep, which meant she was about chest deep. The sandy bottom continued out to where we were standing.

Livi punched me in the arm and switched positions with me so that she was closer to shore than I was. "Ass."

"There is nothing in this lake to be scared of. I've been coming here my whole life. And don't even tell me that this cold water doesn't feel amazing after that hike." I circled around her, blocking her from shore.

She switched positions with me again.

"Why do you keep doing that?" I put my hands on my hips. "Are you going to try to make a break for the beach?"

"No. I want you farther out than I am. That way if something attacks, it'll get you first." She didn't seem like she was joking.

"Aren't you as sweet as pie?" I sank down in the water up to my shoulders. "You want to know the best thing about lake water?"

"Flesh-eating bacteria?"

I gave her an annoyed look and reached for her legs. I wrapped her ankles around my hips. "No one can see what you are doing."

I watched her, carefully, looking for signs that she was uncomfortable or that I was taking it too far in front of her friends. But, because life had always been kind to me, she smiled as she wrapped her legs tighter around me before leaning back in the water. I was instantly hard. In my mind I pictured carrying her back to shore, spreading out a blanket, and eating her for lunch. We stayed like that, connected, talking about nothing and everything until Cole came over and shoved my head under the water.

"Come on, Tay, let's play some football."

Livi untangled her legs from mine, stole the ball cap off my head with a wicked grin, and headed back to shore.

I jumped on Cole's back, dunking him, pissed off he interrupted my time with Livi. When he sputtered to the surface, I shook my head then punched his shoulder. He knew what he did, and he knew he deserved it.

Absentmindedly, I played ball with him and Bailey, but my gaze kept searching out Livi. I couldn't help myself. Maybe I really was enamored. Nah, I was only acting like a such a pussy because I hadn't been in hers yet. Once this weekend was over, I'd be back to my normal awesome self.

She had spread out a towel and was sitting next to Kasey. They talked for a while but then she put my cap on and lay down. Seeing her stretched out like that, her body glistening in the sun, it was like the beginning of the little fantasy I'd had earlier. I fought the urge to go lie next to her for as long as I could, which was all of maybe ten minutes.

I made my way back to shore then sat next to her, leaning in and dripping water on her chest. "Are you sleeping?"

"I was."

"Are you going to make a habit of stealing my clothes?" I couldn't deny I loved seeing her wear my old faded ball cap like I loved seeing her in my tank top yesterday. I needed to lock these sappy emotions down.

"Maybe."

I shook my hair, splattering her with more water droplets. "Wake up. Talk to me."

"No." She moved my cap so I could see her face. "Someone kept me up all night." She sounded irritated, but peeking out beneath the brim of my cap I saw her teasing smile.

I crossed my arms over my bent knees and contemplated the lake. "Explain to me why chicks have this innate need to cuddle?"

Livi scoffed. "You're joking, right? You were the one who wanted to spoon."

I peered down at her, grinning. "Yeah, well, tonight I wanna fork."

She laughed a good, real, perfect laugh. "You're crazy."

I looked back at the water, watching her friends swim and play football. No one was around us, no one could hear anything we were saying, and I wondered if they knew I wanted her. That looking at her, hearing her laugh caused my heart to race and my dick to twitch. I lay down next to her on the sand, which was hot and scratchy on my back. "Don't act like you'll turn me down, sugar. We both know you won't."

She smirked and muttered, "You're cocky too."

"Livi, look at me." I waited until she lifted the cap off her face and then turned, rolling her eyes as she propped herself up on her side. "I want you. For the rest of the weekend I want to own you. I want to make you feel so good that no other man will ever measure up."

She chuckled. "Those are some lofty aspirations, kid." I hated when she shot "kid" at me to keep me at arm's length. No matter, her eyes gave her away. Those beautiful green eyes grew dark, and I could see her pulse beating wildly in her neck.

She could deny it all she wanted, but I was turning her on. Livi liked the unapologetic way I wanted her.

Chapter Twelve

Livi

We were all gathered on the back porch sipping on ice-cold beer and listening to a whole lot of Jack Johnson. It was a movie-perfect setting. The guys made us lunch and then set us up, ordering us to relax while they cleaned the kitchen. Hiring these two men was the best idea Bailey ever had. None of us had moved for an hour.

Now, on the other side of the porch, Kasey, Allie, and Bailey were playing cards. Cole was inside doing something on his laptop, and Taylor was sitting next to me, studying. He looked hot as hell in his glasses, no shirt, with a pencil at his lips. He was right; I wouldn't deny him. I should, but I wouldn't. It'd been too long since I'd felt wanted.

Patrick and I had been having problems long before I caught him banging his secretary on his desk. Aside from the cheating, what had he been thinking? I mean with all the #MeToo why wasn't he worried he was buying a sexual harassment lawsuit—blondie couldn't believe he would be faithful to her if he was doing her and had a wife. The point really was he didn't care. Not about me, her, or anyone but himself and him being able to do what he wanted when he wanted to do it.

Ultimately, I didn't think he'd cheated because he fell in love with someone else, or because he fell out of love with me. We'd been drifting apart for a while, and it's sad to say, but I didn't make any effort to fix it. We weren't an "us" for so long, I'd gone on with my life without him while sharing our house occasionally since he was never home. When I found him doing his secretary in his office, I was pissed and felt betrayed, but after I'd kicked him out—that was a scene I never wanted to repeat again: him begging, me screaming, him begging, me throwing his clothes out the front door, him begging and me threatening to call the cops—I realized I didn't really care all that much. I didn't think I was losing anything I wanted to hold on to. That's when I knew for sure things were over.

The fact my marriage had ended was easy to keep from the people close to me because its demise didn't affect me all that much. I was used to doing all the day-to-day stuff by myself. Patrick was rarely around the last couple of years. I knew it was time to tell my friends though. Maybe I'd share on Sunday. That way I wouldn't mess up our girls' weekend. Or maybe I'd shoot them a long text once we were all home. Then turn off my phone for a few hours. Or days.

"Penny for your thoughts, sugar?" Taylor reached over and stroked my thigh with the eraser end of his pencil. It made my breath hitch in my chest. One touch from him and my blood was pumping double time.

Before I could answer, Cole came out the back door and let out an obnoxiously loud yawn. "All right, ladies, what's the game plan for tonight? Want to go out to dinner, or want to eat in? You tell us. We work for you."

Bailey answered for all of us. I didn't want to call her bossy, because women weren't bossy, they took charge and got shit done. She'd been that way as long as I'd known her. The first day we met in an ethics class freshman year, she'd basically told the TA he didn't know what he was talking about and had taken over teaching the planned lesson. Baily always knew what she wanted, and she never backed down from it. I admired that about her. "I was thinking we could go into town early and walk around, maybe do some shopping. Then head to dinner. Are there any bars in town?"

"There's one. It's small and Friday nights aren't all that bumping here. If you guys wait 'til tomorrow night to hit the bar, they usually have live music." Cole swatted at a fly that landed on the table with the switch he'd been holding.

Kasey flicked the dead fly off and watched it sail to the ground. "That sounds good to me. We can do some touristy stuff tonight and then tomorrow we'll go out on the town."

Bailey stood, stretching her arms over her head. "Okay, I'm going to go shower the lake water off. You guys don't need to come into town with us if you don't want to. We'll wait 'til we get home to start drinking."

Allie scoffed, taking another sip from her wineglass. "Speak for yourself, woman."

I got to my feet, following Bailey into the house, the AC making chill bumps erupt on my arms. She threw me a bottle of water from the fridge. "Each of these inside bedrooms has a shower. The owner left instructions that we can all shower at the same time and the hot water will still work."

I unscrewed the cap off my water. "Okay, I'll use the one in the guys' room."

"Hey, Livi?"

I spun around dramatically making her smile. "Yeeeessss?"

"Are you... I mean, you and... Is everything okay?"

I took a deep breath and held it. I could come clean right now. I *should* come clean and tell Bailey everything. She obviously knew something was up. The more time I spent around Taylor, the more relaxed I became. We flirted and touched, and I was sure it looked completely inappropriate. But for some reason, I couldn't do it. I couldn't open my mouth and tell her that my marriage was over. I wasn't ready for my failed relationship to be the center of attention.

I let out that breath, and said in my perky voice, "Yeah, everything is fine."

Bailey stared at me, not blinking. She knew I was keeping something from her, but before she could call me on it, Kasey walked in. "I'm going to shower too. The guys said they are going to stay here if we're sure we don't need them."

Bailey answered Kasey without taking her assessing gaze off me. "Yeah, we're good. I'll drive. Allie can get as crazy as she wants."

Allie came skipping into the house, letting the porch door slam shut behind her. "Did I hear my name?"

"Yeah, you lush. I was telling Kasey that I would drive us tonight."

Allie immediately started singing *Addicted to Love* and making herself a cocktail with a lot of flourish and finesse. I used the entertaining distraction to my advantage, grabbing my stuff and heading into the bathroom off the guys' room. I shut and locked the door. The last thing I needed was Taylor coming in here.

Bailey was already suspicious. I didn't need to add fuel to the fire. I took my time, letting the hot water wash away the day and the tension in my muscles. I adored my friends, and we'd been close for a lot of years, but that meant that they knew me as well as I knew them. They knew when I wasn't being myself. It was only a matter of time before one of them cornered me and demanded I come clean.

After I was done, I towel dried my hair and got dressed into my outfit for the evening. When I opened the door, Taylor was lying on the bottom bunk. His chiseled chest was still bare, his skin even darker from the time he'd spent out in sun by the lake. His shorts were lying low, his hips on display.

He was gorgeous, and so damn tempting.

He was also pouting. "You locked the door."

I nodded. "I was in the shower."

"I wanted to be in the shower with you." He sat up, turning to place his bare feet on the floor.

My smile was tight. "I know, that's why I locked the door."

He held his hand out for me, silently asking me to come to him. My head told me to leave the room. We could hang out tonight after everyone was asleep. It was safer that way. "Taylor, I need to finish getting ready. I don't want everyone to be waiting on me. Bailey gets super pissy about stuff like that."

He gestured for me with his outstretched hand, not giving up. "Come here, just for a second." The truth was, no matter how stupid it was, I wanted to go to him. Taylor made me want to throw caution to the wind, he made me want to be as wild as he was.

I made a show that I was reluctant to cross the room, glancing at the bedroom door to make sure it was still closed.

Weak. I was a weak woman. Taylor grabbed both of my hands and dragged me between his thighs. When he looked up at me with such intense desire shining in his eyes, my stomach dropped. He pulled me down for a kiss. It was slow and deep, his tongue making lazy passes over mine. It made me want to lose myself in him, to climb onto the bed and say the hell with everything else. Everything and everyone.

Which was why I pulled away.

"What's wrong, sugar, you look stressed."

I shrugged, licking his taste from my lips. "Bailey asked me what was going on earlier. She knows something's up. I don't want to tell them about Patrick and me until Sunday. You and I... I think we're becoming obvious, Taylor. You're going to have to back off. No more touching or sexual innuendos. I don't want my friends to think I'm being unfaithful even for a couple of days. It'll stress them out. They'll worry about me, and I want them to relax and have fun."

"Livi, I... No."

I jerked away from him, my hands going to my hips. "What do you mean *no*? You promised me that you would back off if I asked you to. This is me asking."

"I like you. I like touching you and even more importantly, *you* like it when I touch you. Don't try to deny it. I can see what I do to you." He reached for my hand, guiding it shamelessly to his dick, making me grab his length. He was hard, and mouthwateringly long. "This is what you do to me."

I pulled my hand away, shaking my head. "Taylor, how many times do I have to explain this to you? I'm not a kid anymore. I'm an adult with responsibilities and friends who value marriage. Friends who will be disappointed in me if they think I'm cheating."

He scrubbed his hands down his face, exasperated. "Who cares what they think? It's only for a couple of days. You can tell them on Sunday."

Oh no he didn't. That sounded like something Patrick would say. All about him, damn how it affected anyone else.

"*I* care." I pointed to myself. "Look, I'm not telling you we have to stop. I'm telling you to watch yourself around Allie and Bailey, and honor my wishes not to hurt my friends."

I *should* be telling him to stop though. That was the grown-up, mature thing to do. No, the grown-up, mature thing to do would have been to tell my friends months ago that I was getting divorced. I kept reminding Taylor that I was an adult, but maybe the person who needed convincing was myself.

"Livi. Dammit." He was at war with himself on this one. I could tell by the different looks flittering across his face. But in this I wouldn't back down. My friends' opinion of me mattered and I refused to let them think that I would cheat. I wouldn't. I'd never lower myself to Patrick's standards. Finally, Taylor grabbed my hands in his again. "You're right, and I'm sorry. I promise, I'll be more discreet around your friends."

"Thank you."

I leaned down and gave him a quick peck before walking out of the room. The only problem was, I didn't want to walk out of the room. I wanted to climb onto his lap and grind against him. It was a good thing we were going into town without him and Cole tonight. I needed some space. I needed to put some distance between myself and Taylor.

This fling had barely started and it was already too intense.

Chapter Thirteen

Taylor

I was going crazy. The girls had been gone for too long. I missed Livi. I had known this girl for less than twenty-four hours and I fucking *missed* her. What in the holy hell was wrong with me? I needed to man up. I was being a giant pussy. I ran my hands through my hair, frustrated. Cole stepped out onto the front porch. That's right, I was sitting on the front porch waiting for her to get home like an eager puppy. Like a fucking loyal dog. He handed me another beer; I was going through them like water at this point.

"Hey, man, you, uh, you okay?" He plopped down in the chair opposite me, a Jack and Coke in his hands. Jack and Coke was pretty much all Cole drank after sundown. He had a lot of rules for himself, as opposed to me. I thought rules were the harbinger of doom.

I took a long pull off the fresh bottle. "I'm fine."

"Yeah? You seem just peachy." Cole gestured to the three empty bottles at my feet. "Man, she's just a chick like the thousands of other chicks you've bagged."

"Thousands? I'm good, but I'm not *that* good." I laughed humorlessly. "I don't know what's happening to me. I feel like a little bitch. I fucking spooned her all night last night. Like wrapped my body around hers and slept like a damn baby. She told me today that I needed to back off, that her friends were asking questions. It killed me to say okay. I don't want to back off. I want to tell her friends everything, I want to be able to touch her and kiss her and flirt with her out in the open." I ran my hands through my hair again, pulling it straight up.

Cole started to laugh, like side-splitting laugh. "Aww, man, Tay, you're into her. You actually *like* a girl. Hell, it only took twenty-eight years." He wiped at his eyes. "Of course you had to pick a girl that lives four states away. Not to mention, she's technically still married. Good job, bro."

I looked at him like he was a mental patient. "You're crazy. I don't *like* her. I want to nail her, I *need* to nail her. The need to nail her is all encompassing. That's all. Once I get it out of my system I'll feel better."

"Oh yeah? All encompassing? When's the last time you cuddled because you wanted to?" Cole took a large gulp of his drink and then crunched noisily on some ice.

I glared at him, trying to harm him with my mind like a Jedi. He knew the answer to that. I didn't cuddle. I didn't spoon. I didn't sleep over. Cole had known me since we were eighteen-year-old douche bags. He knew the way I operated.

"I get it, Tay. Livi's hot, she's funny, and she has a body that won't quit. But she lives in another state, man, and she's also going through a divorce. I meant what I said yesterday, she's not for you." Cole shrugged like what he told me was no big deal when really his statements were irritating as fuck. "You want her this weekend? Fine. But you better get it through your head that that's all you're going to get."

"That's all I need." Right? Or was *Cole* right? Was Livi the first girl to ever get under my skin? Whatever. Even if she was, it was most likely because I couldn't have her. She was unattainable. I'm a dude, we want what we can't have. My life was golden. Everything was going according to plan. This was nothing more than a weekend fling. I was going to be fine, not changed forever from having met the gorgeous blonde bombshell who wrote sex scenes for a living.

Cole and I sat on the porch drinking and shooting the shit until we saw headlights pull into the driveway. A smile took over my entire face and my heart started to race. *Really, heart? Do you really need to be that excited to see Livi?* I glanced over at Cole, to see if he knew my traitorous heart was pounding out of my chest.

The girls climbed out of the car laughing. My gaze searched for Livi as I stood. "Y'all have fun?"

Allie answered me. "This town is fucking adorable. We met some locals at dinner, they told us the band playing at the bar tomorrow night is actually pretty good." She shut her car door. "Said it gets packed, that we should try to head there a little early so we can get a table."

I held the screen door open for them. "Of course, ladies. It's your world, we just work here."

Cole opened the front door, leading them inside and heading to the bar they'd set up yesterday. "Who wants a drink?" They all raised their hands as they filed inside.

He stood at the bar and clapped his palms together once. "Who wants what? Wait. Let me try to guess first. Allie and Livi want vodka Sprite with a splash of cranberry and a lime. Kasey wants a whiskey and Coke, and Ms. Bailey wants a shot of tequila with a beer chaser. Am I right?"

Cole had always been better at the details than me. I was more entertainment, and he was more manners and service with a smile. We were a good team and more often than not, we were paired together. My mom thought my little side hustle was as close to prostitution as one could safely get, and my dad ignored it altogether because he knew I only did it to piss him off. Cole hid his part-time job from his overly moral yet supportive parents.

Bailey perched her butt on top of the bar, reaching for the bottle of Patron. "You are correct, sir."

I stared at Livi from across the room. I knew she was avoiding my gaze. Trying to ignore me all together. I guess she'd meant what she said earlier. No big deal, I needed to keep my distance until bedtime. I could do that. I wasn't that big of a lost cause.

"Okay, what now? Y'all wanna have another dance party in the living room? Go for a midnight swim? Play some cards? Your wish is our command." I threw my arm around Allie's shoulder. *See?* I could act like there was nothing going on with Livi and me. I was friendly with everyone. It was my personality, not an obsession with one gorgeous girl.

Kasey tasted her drink, frowned at Cole, and then added more whiskey to the top. "Let's go for a swim."

Bailey threw back her shot and then nodded. "I'm down for a swim, what good is a private dock if we don't use it at least once while we're here."

I smiled like the cat that ate the fucking canary then licked his paws clean. "Everyone else good with that?" I asked everyone, but I meant Livi. I had a hankering to see that girl dripping wet and wearing next to nothing in the moonlight. I waited until I saw her nod before asking, "Lake then?"

Predictably, Livi made a case for swimming in the safety of the pool, but she was vetoed by Bailey. "Come on, Liv. We can swim in a pool whenever we want. When do we get the chance to go for a midnight swim in a lake? Never."

Allie pursed her lips. "That's true, Livi. We won't let any lake monsters pull you under. Promise."

I laughed, pointing at the object of my seemingly unwavering affection. "Okay, Livi, looks like you're outnumbered. Lake time." She shot daggers at me from across the room. I didn't care. I was minutes away from having a sexy girl in a bikini in the middle of a dark deserted lake. It was every man's dream come true.

Every man's dream and a scene in most horror movies ever made.

Chapter Fourteen

Livi

They wanted to go swimming in the lake, in the dark. I needed another drink. I knew what Taylor's end game was. During dinner Bailey had brought up how attentive he was with me. I had kept my cool and explained it away as nothing. I told my friends that maybe he was a little flirty, but it was going to help me write my next book. His one-liners and sexual innuendos were a romance writer's dream. They had all laughed about it and the subject was thankfully dropped.

But two vodka drinks in, and a dark sexy scary lake meant things were about to get complicated. Between the alcohol and Taylor being Taylor, my inhibitions were down enough for me not to care.

Stupid, stupid me, I had thought about Taylor the whole time we were gone. I wanted him. I wanted to feel desired *by* him. I longed to be touched by someone who was into me. I couldn't remember the last time I felt that from Patrick. Damn. This was going to happen. This simmering thing between the two of us was going to boil over. I needed to keep a clear head long enough to get away from my friends' prying eyes.

I changed into my suit and threw Taylor's tank top over it. Might as well start turning him on now. See? Stupid.

I came out of my room and immediately felt Taylor's gaze on me. I could feel the heat coming from him, warming me to the core. I shivered with anticipation.

He stalked over, handing me a fresh drink as he whispered next to my ear, "I was planning on behaving in front of your friends, but I doubt I'll be able to control myself now that you're wearing my shirt."

"Well, I'll just have to take it off then, won't I?" I took a sip of my expertly made cocktail, grateful that at least Cole did his actual job so Bailey would have nothing to complain about.

Taylor chuckled. "All right, sugar, how many drinks did you have at dinner?"

I smiled what I hoped was a sexy smile. "Enough to make tonight interesting." Then I walked away to join my friends on the back porch, appearing cooler and unaffected than I actually was. Inside I was a shaking live wire waiting for the next moment Taylor Hill decided to touch me. I craved his attention.

We followed the narrow path down to the dock in a single-file line, Bailey leading because she no longer trusted Taylor's navigational skills. The lake looked so peaceful in the moonlight. The stars were reflected in the smooth black surface of the water. With everyone around me and the alcohol running through my veins, things didn't look as scary as I thought they would. Instead the water was inviting, the darkness seductive.

Once we reached the dock, I peeled off Taylor's shirt and let it slide out of my fingers to fall onto the ground next to my empty cup. I stepped silently out toward the edge. I could hear my friends laughing in the background, but I knew Taylor would follow me. Like I knew the instant he stepped up behind me, sensing him even before he placed his hand on my bare hip. Goose bumps spread all over my body, welcoming his touch.

"You ready, sugar?"

I turned to him, a smirk on my face, playing my part. "Promise not to let the monsters get me?"

He nodded and grabbed my hand as we jumped into the water side by side. I had given him a big speech only hours before, telling him to back off, telling him to watch himself around my friends, and here I was, throwing caution to the wind.

I wanted his hands on me as much as I wanted his attention on me. We swam in the direction of the shoreline until we were about waist deep and stopped, sinking down in the lakebed, letting the cool water hit our shoulders.

Taylor reached for me under the surface, dragging me toward him through the black water. "You okay? You haven't been this quiet since I met you." He smiled, turning us so that my back was to the shore and he was in position to get eaten by monstrous lake creatures first.

"I'm fine." I bit at my lip, owning up to what happened between us. "I'm sorry about earlier, before we left for town. It's not all you, obviously, I'm as much to blame."

I let him pick up my legs and wrap them around his waist. I felt his hard length pressed up against my core. Against my better judgment I tightened my hold, grinding against him as slowly as I could, trying my best not to make ripples in the water. I grinned when he closed his eyes and clenched his sharp jaw.

"You were right, Taylor. I love it when you touch me. I crave it."

He opened his eyes; the moon was bright enough for me to see the lust that filled them. "I crave you too, sugar. More than I have ever craved anyone. I need to have you. I'm selfish and I'm a bastard. When this is all over, I'll take you to the airport and never look back. But tonight, this weekend... I want all of you."

I swallowed, audibly. His words made me ache. I wanted to be in our little bed, on the porch where the fan would drown out my moans. "Okay."

"Okay?"

"For the rest of the weekend, I'm yours. All yours. As much and as often as we can manage, you can have me." I ground against him again, hard and slow, driving myself wild in the process.

"My friends can't know. When this trip is over, so is this little fling."

Chapter Fifteen

Taylor

My cock strained against my swim trunks, begging to be let out to play. My blood felt like lava running through my veins despite the cool lake water. I wanted to pick Livi up, throw her over my shoulder, and fucking sprint back to the house. I wanted Livi, and I wanted her *now*. I didn't care anymore that I was pathetic. I didn't care that I was too obsessed with her. None of that mattered. All of it was fucking next week's problem. She said I could have her, and every second between now and the moment I sank inside her would be pure torture.

I groaned when I saw everyone make their way over to us, interrupting the building tension. Livi laughed and pulled away from me, and I missed her instantly. Call me a pussy, it didn't matter anymore. I was Taylor Hill, a legend about to meet his match.

Allie swam up and handed Livi her drink. "Here you go, Livi Lou. I saw you slammed yours on the walk down here. We can share mine."

I narrowed my eyes on that red plastic cup. I didn't want Livi to drink anymore. I wanted her sober. I wanted her to remember every ounce of pleasure I planned on making her feel once we got back to the house.

"Thanks, Allie cat." Livi took a big gulp of the drink and I nudged her under the water.

Kasey squealed, "Oh my god. Something just brushed against my leg."

Oops, wrong chick.

"Kasey, it was probably a fish," I said. "Calm down or Livi is going to start crying."

That earned me a kick, but I knew it was coming. I grabbed Livi's leg and held on. I ran my hand up her thigh and brushed my fingers against her pussy. I smiled smugly when her eyes closed in response to my touch. She was so responsive, so—

Suddenly I found myself under water. I came up sputtering, and Cole was on me. Dunking me. Again.

When he finally let me keep my head above water, he mumbled, "Stop looking at Livi like you want to eat her. You're being too obvious." He let me go and swam back over to the girls, positioning himself between me and *my* girl. "Let's play a game."

I grinned. "Hide-and-seek?" Cole shot me a glare and Livi snorted.

"How about I Never?" Bailey suggested.

Kasey, Allie, and Livi all groaned in unison.

"What? Y'all don't want to play?" Bailey looked irritated. "What else are we going to play wading out in the middle of a lake? We have no cards, no dice…"

Cole raised his drink overhead. "I'll play. So will Tay. He loves this game. He gets shitfaced every time. There's not much this guy hasn't tried at least once."

I sent water splashing in Cole's direction. He covered his drink with his hand, raising it higher up above the water. "Dude, quit it. You're going to get lake water in my Jack."

Livi had a serious look on her face as she shook her head. "No joke, Tay. Cole could get dysentery."

I chuckled, rolling my eyes. "No flesh-eating bacteria, no dysentery, no monsters. Stop worrying so much, sugar."

Bailey's eyebrows raised so high they disappeared into her hair line. "'Sugar'?"

Livi laughed nervously. "He's Southern, Bailey, not trying to get into my pants." Her voice sounded strained, Her unease apparent. I reached down and placed my hand on her hip, trying to calm her without anyone noticing.

Bailey kept her eyes on me, so I smiled as cheekily as I could, giving nothing away. She must have gotten over it 'cause she said, "Let's play. Who wants to go first?"

Allie raised her hand. "Me."

Livi sighed and let her head fall back until her face was turned to the night sky. She huffed under her breath, "Good lord, here we go." I grabbed her hand under the water. Standing here, this close to her, watching her laugh and smile, and watching her beautiful breasts covered in water?

Torture.

My dick was crying.

Allie spoke again, happily starting the game that not many people seemed to want to play. "Never have I ever had a threesome."

Damn. I took a drink, but to my relief so did Cole. I searched my memory, was he lying? Nope, that was right. Halloween sophomore year. The nurse and the cheerleader. Roommates.

When Cole offered to go next, I cringed.

"Never have I ever kissed a dude. So, for y'all, drink if you've kissed another girl."

All four of them looked down, up, anywhere but at each other as they drank. Hmm my sad dick gave a little twitch at the thought of them making out. I'm a guy, sue me.

Kasey's turn. "Never have I ever got so drunk that I didn't remember what I did the night before."

Everyone drank except for Kasey, which made her smile smugly. Petty one point for what I knew of that one. She was a little holier than thou.

Livi grabbed Allie's cup and held it over head. "Never have I ever got so wasted I fell into a trash can." That must have had its desired effect because Kasey stuck her tongue out at Livi and then drank. But so did Cole.

I looked at him like I was sorely disappointed in his behavior. "Really, dude? A trash can?"

He shrugged. "Freshman year."

I nodded in understanding. We were all lightweights at eighteen. "I'll go. Never have I ever..." Damn it was hard thinking of something to say without having to drink myself. "...paid for sex."

No one drank.

Bailey snorted and shook her head. "Never have I ever asked someone to pull my hair during sex."

Cole drank. Wow, I was learning a lot about my friend tonight. You'd think after all these years of constant partying together, I'd know his sexual preferences better. I looked away from him in time to see Livi bring Allie's cup away from her lips. "Whoa, wait a minute. Livi, did you just drink to that? You like to have your hair pulled?"

She ignored me and turned to Allie, letting her know it was once again her turn. Allie tapped her chin, her smile taking on an extremely wicked gleam. "Never have I ever asked someone to cho—"

Livi cut Allie off by sending a wave of lake water sailing into her face. "That's enough."

Kasey and Bailey were cracking up, leaning on each other like they needed help staying upright. Livi sounded pissed but she was still wearing a hint of a grin so she couldn't honestly be that mad.

"What was that about? What was Allie going to say?" Please god let it be what I thought it was. I mean, so many of my prayers had already come true over the last twenty-four hours, but one more wouldn't hurt.

Livi shook her head, pointing a finger at her friend. "Nope. Don't even think about it, Allie cat. I can play dirty too."

Allie kept that evil smirk on her face. "Oh Livi, it's okay. No one here is going to judge you for liking it a little rough." She motioned in my direction. "I'm sure Tay here is a freak in the sheets. He'd probably applaud you."

Livi snatched the drink they had been sharing and downed it in one long gulp. The sight of her swallowing made my dick jerk again. Man, I was pathetic when it came to that girl.

"*No mas* for you, Allie cat. You are white girl wasted." Livi turned to face her other two friends. "And you two. Stop it. You're only encouraging her. I have dirt on y'all as well."

Kasey and Baily were still laughing, but Kasey leaned over and pulled Livi into a hug. "Aww, Livi, we love you."

I narrowed my eyes, silently begging my dick to calm down. At this rate, I'd have to stay in the cold water for a few minutes after everyone headed back to shore. Flirting with Livi was one thing, but walking out with raging wood was another. Bailey fucking noticed everything, and my dick was hard to miss. Ha. See what I did there?

But alas, I was a glutton for all things Livi related, so I refused to give up. "You know, secrets don't make friends. Are y'all going to share with the rest of us?" I needed to know exactly how rough my girl liked it before I got her back in bed. I was a glutton, but I also aimed only to please.

Bailey splashed water in my face. "No, secrets don't make friends, but they do *keep* them."

Bailey. Ruining my good time since two days ago.

Chapter Sixteen

Livi

My friends were skating on thin ice. *Never have I ever* was not a good time. It always ended with us calling each other out until we were all so bombed we couldn't walk straight. Ten-plus years of experiences and friendship made that a dangerous game.

Allie, Kasey, Bailey, and Cole were racing out to the middle of the lake to a floating dock that seemed to belong to someone else. Loser had to run back up to the house to grab the towels that we'd all forgotten to bring with us. It was the middle of summer in southern Georgia, but getting out of the lake water was going to be chilly any way you sliced it.

I was happy to be alone with Taylor at the moment, although I knew he was going to demand to know what my friends had been giving me a hard time about. He hauled me to him, running his hands across my stomach and hips and ass under the cover of the black water.

"Come on, sugar, tell me." He brought his mouth close to my ear, whispering, "Tell me how you like to be fucked."

I pulled away from him, but I couldn't help the chills that raced down my spine. I took a deep breath. Good thing I was well on my way to drunk and my inhibitions were extremely low. "I may like it a little, uh, rougher, than my friends, but that's not saying much. They're all prudes. Even Allie, although she talks a big game."

Taylor's face broke out into a devilish grin. His hand dipped in between my thighs, rubbing my clit through my bikini bottoms. My breath hitched in my throat, need for him rendering me breathless. "How rough, Livi?"

"Does it matter?"

"It sure as hell does. You're mine, remember? I want to make sure I give you *everything* you want this weekend."

I knew I was most likely blushing. I wrote about sex all the time, but for some reason talking to Taylor like this was making me feel all feverish and flushed.

"Tay, honestly I can't stand out here and talk to you about this. My friends are drunk, not stupid. If they overheard us—"

"They're halfway across the lake with their heads underwater. There is no way they can hear anything we're saying."

I shook my head.

Taylor narrowed his eyes and sank down in the water to his neck. He reached out and grabbed my hips, pulling me deeper into the lake, my pelvis flush against his body, holding me in place with his hands on my ass. I let out a little whimper, showing more of my cards than I'd intended to. It was hard to appear cool in front of the playboy that was Taylor Hill.

His grin went from devilish to satisfied, clearly loving the effect he had on me. "What if I try to guess what you like? Every time I guess right, you give me a little reward. Deal?"

I wanted him to keep touching me. I wanted to reward him so fucking bad. My friends needed to get bored of swimming ASAP. It was time for bed.

"Allie already mentioned the hair pulling. Let's see, wrists pinned above your head?"

I ground my hips against his. Rubbing my core against his cock, making him bite his lip. I hadn't been sure what kind of reward he'd been after, but he seemed to like the one I'd come up with.

"Good girl. A little dirty talk? You like to be told how good you feel? You like to be told what to do? Harder, faster."

I used my legs to hold him tighter, circling my hips again. He breathed the word *fuck* under his breath.

"Up against the wall? Any wall will do."

I gave a quick thrust.

"My hand at your throat enough for a little bit of pressure, a little glimpse of the wild side?"

I reached under the water, palming his cock in my hand, rubbing up and down.

His eyes sparkled in the moonlight. "That's good to hear, sugar, because that's exactly how I like it too."

Chapter Seventeen

Taylor

We were finally back at the house. Thank god. I haven't dry humped as much as Livi and I have this weekend since I was a freshman in high school. I was the one who started that little game in the water, but I had ended up seconds away from blowing my load in the lake. Good to know my girl liked it rough. I did too, I hadn't been lying. I wasn't into S and M or anything like that, but I liked a slight edge to my sex. Enough to keep things interesting.

I looked across the room at Livi; she was laughing at Bailey and Allie. They were once again drunk and dancing. Kasey and Cole were at the bar taking turns trying to catch Cheetos in their mouths after tossing them in the air. I needed all these people to go to bed. Now.

As if reading my mind Livi let out a super fake yawn. "Wiped, y'all. I'm going to bed. 'Night." She turned without waiting for a response and went out onto the side porch.

I watched until the door shut and I could no longer see her. Then, I was suddenly beamed in the head. I looked over to see Cole snickering behind his hand. Inebriated jackass.

"Did you throw a Cheeto at my head?"

Kasey giggled. "I think it's still called a Cheetosssss." She emphasized the "s" for an extra ten seconds. "Even though it's only one." Cole nodded solemnly, like this was an important fact.

I rolled my eyes. "What? Cheeto is the singular for Cheetos."

Kasey shook her head. "No. I'm ninety-nine percent sure it's still Cheetos. We can look it up though."

I held up my hand to stop her when she pulled her phone out of her pocket. "No thanks. I don't really care one way or another. I'm going to bed."

Kasey shrugged. "Suit yourself." She and Cole started throwing Cheetos at Bailey and Allie as they danced around the kitchen. They were making it rain with cheese puffs. Wow, Cole was fall-in-the-trash-can wasted.

I thought about cutting everyone off and sending them to bed. If they kept drinking, they were going to be hurting tomorrow for sure. Before I could tell them to head out, Livi came walking out of Cole's and my room—she was like a ninja, I hadn't even seen her go in there—wearing one of my t-shirts and a pair of tiny sleep shorts. My mind was made up in about two seconds flat. Screw wrangling those drunk assholes, I had a girl waiting on me to pull her pretty blonde hair.

I ran into the bathroom and showered as quickly as I could. I brushed my teeth and threw on a pair of workout shorts. When I went back into the living room, I cringed. Cole was up on the table and Bailey was teaching him how to "dougie." If Livi wasn't so damn tempting, I would have gotten out my phone and videoed this throwback hilarity.

Quietly, I slipped out the back door and went around the side of the house. I tripped twice. Once over a stick and once over what I was almost positive was a live raccoon. I let myself in through the screen door and latched it behind me.

"Oh my gosh, Taylor, are you okay?"

Eyes closed, I tried to steady my rapid breathing, I had run the whole way. The raccoon had scared the crap out of me. "Yeah, I'm good. I, uh, tripped."

"You have a pinecone in your hair."

I patted my head until I found it and then tossed it to the ground. When I opened my eyes, my breathing became erratic for a whole new reason.

Livi looked sexy as hell. Her damp hair was piled on top of her head, her face was free of makeup, and she was not only wearing my t-shirt, she was wearing her glasses as well. Her laptop was sitting open on her bare legs. I watched as she closed it and placed it on the small nightstand beside the bed.

"Are you going to stand there and stare all night?"

I started to stalk toward her. "You're beautiful."

She laughed lightly, her cheeks turning pink. "Thank you." She ran her hands over the tops of her smooth tanned thighs. "Turn on the fan."

I knew I was grinning like an idiot, but *turn on the fan* basically meant *make me scream*. I flipped on the large fan and launched myself onto the bed, making her laugh again, which was becoming one of my favorite sounds in the world.

"Ready to fork so hard?" Her laughter faded away; her face became serious, guarded. I reached over and placed my hand on her hip. "Hey. What's with the sad face? Tell me what's running through that head of yours."

When she answered me, all her words came out in a rush. "I, um, I haven't been with anyone else since my ex and even then, we hadn't slept together in a long time. I mean...you're used to twenty-year-old co-eds and—"

Gently, I put my palm over her mouth. "I understand what you are trying to say, Livi. I will go as slow as you need me to. I will make sure that every single thing I do brings you pleasure. As far as the other chicks...you are the sexiest, most beautiful woman I have ever met. Stop thinking and let go. The only thing that matters right now is this."

I sat up, took her face in my hands, and kissed her with everything I had, trying to show her how irresistible and desirable she was with that kiss.

Then I leaned back against the headboard and pulled her into my lap. Her hot little body was straddling mine, her pussy rubbing on my cock looking for release. When her grinding became too much, felt too good, I flipped us over. I pinned her to the bed with my body.

Taking both her small wrists in one hand, I pushed them against the mattress. She moaned. I used my other hand to reach between us, rubbing her clit through her lacy thong. "So wet for me, sugar." I ran my teeth along her jaw, nibbled on her neck. I was all for taking my time, savoring our first time together, but she had other ideas.

Livi bit down on my shoulder, sucking lightly. "Tay, please..." She arched into my hand, begging me for more.

I sat up and pulled my shirt off her body and then ripped her panties down and threw them aside. She whimpered and raked her nails down my chest. I trailed two fingers between her breasts, down her stomach, and through her folds before dipping them inside her.

"Oh god, sugar, you feel so perfect. Tell me what you want, Livi."

She answered by pushing my shorts down and freeing my cock. She took me in her hands and began stroking me. A stroke down and twist back up, stroke down and twist back up. I groaned against her neck, pushing her back down on the bed with my hips. "Tell me, Livi."

She arched up, capturing my mouth with hers. She took my lower lip in her teeth, and then licked the sting away. Lying back against the pillows, she looked up at me and without breaking eye contact said, "Fuck me, Taylor."

Holy. Shit.

I reached over to the nightstand and grabbed the condom I'd put there when I came in, rolling it on. I nudged her thighs apart, settling my hips on top of hers and positioning the head of my dick at her entrance. I wanted more than anything to drive into her, but I told her I'd be careful. I promised she'd feel only pleasure with me, and I'd meant it. I inched into her body, slowly. She was tight, and she felt so damn good.

"Livi, oh god, baby." I rested my forehead against hers, panting. "Are you okay?"

She nodded, almost franticly. "I'm okay. Keep going. Please don't stop."

I chuckled. "Yes ma'am." With one more thrust I was in all the way, buried to the hilt. I started moving inside of her slowly, cautiously. Testing what she could handle. Livi raked her fingers down my back and gripped my ass in both hands. Spreading her legs wider and arching into me.

"Harder, Taylor. I'm okay. I promise."

I shook my head. I didn't trust myself. If I let go, I might end up hurting her. I rolled us over, placing her on top.

"Show me what you need, baby."

Chapter Eighteen

Livi

Show me what you need, baby. I felt chills travel down my spine; whether it was from Taylor's whispered words or the fan hitting my bare back, I didn't know. I wanted to laugh. I had to bite my cheek to keep it from bubbling out. Taylor was amazing, his body, his dick. As sad as it was to say, everything on him and about him was better than the man I had spent the last five years with.

I rode Taylor shamelessly. This was exactly what I'd needed. One weekend with him and all would be right in my world. I let my head fall back as he trailed his hands up my thighs, up over my hips, palming my breasts briefly before placing one hand against my throat. He did it perfectly. He didn't wrap his fingers around, only added the tiniest amount of pressure. I leaned into his touch, trusting him explicably.

"Oh god, oh god, Taylor. Please don't stop."

He moaned. The sound incredibly sexy. "It's all you, sugar. I won't stop until you do, take what you need, baby."

His words combined with the deep Southern timber of his voice and the permission to take all the time I wanted sent me flying over the edge. I screamed. I know I did. I was fairly certain it was loud enough to hear over the fan. When I screamed out his name, I felt Taylor jerk his release, pulsing inside me over and over.

I smiled as I collapsed beside him. "That was…perfect."

Taylor sat on the side of the bed, getting rid of the condom. "It was better than perfect." He lay back down and turned on his side to face me. "I still get you the rest of the weekend, right? Please tell me you haven't changed your mind."

I snuggled up next to him and spoke into his chest. "Are you kidding me? After that? I'm yours. You are exactly what I needed in my life. By Sunday you are going to be tired of nailing me."

He snorted. "Fuck me. Nail me. So dirty and bossy. I like it." He reached out and put his hand on my cheek. "Tell me about your divorce." He didn't really pose it as a question. It was more like a demand. I didn't want to talk about my divorce seconds after he had given me a mind-blowing orgasm. It seemed weird, and out of place. When I stayed silent, Taylor stroked my jaw. "Please, Livi. I want to know you."

That was sweeter than it should have been. The playboy wanted to know the girl he'd made scream his name. Taylor was full of pleasing contradictions.

"You were inside me moments ago and now you want to talk about my ex?"

He nodded, brushing the hair back off my cheek. "Let me in, just a little."

I sighed and thought, why not. This was old news now, and Taylor was mine for a weekend.

"I met Patrick in college at a bar. We dated and fell in love and he asked me to marry him. I said yes because he was sweet and funny and driven." I rolled onto my back, putting my head on Taylor's chest and staring out the screen at the lake. "After we got married, the things I loved about him faded away. All that was left was this money-hungry workaholic. He was never home, he never made space in his life for our marriage. When I'd ask him to spend time with me or go on a date with me, he'd act like I was nothing more than a bothersome, petulant child. After a while, I stopped missing him. Stopped begging him to be with me. When I caught him cheating, I ended things."

Taylor trailed his fingers through my hair. "Your ex sounds like my dad, except my mom is exactly like him. Two money-hungry jerks who never could be bothered to make time for their kid."

"I thought you said you used to vacation here with them. Did they at least spend time with you then?"

He shook his head. "I didn't come here with my parents. They would never spend an extended amount of time away from work like that. I came with friends and their families."

I kissed his pec. "I'm sorry you had shitty parents." I didn't want to tell him about Patrick. I didn't want to ruin our little bliss bubble, but I was glad I did. I felt like maybe we understood each other a little better now.

He kissed the top of my head. "I'm sorry your ex was an asshole." He chuckled. "Although, at the moment, I'm not *that* sorry."

I snorted.

I could feel him smiling against my hair. "All right, sugar, go to sleep. I plan on waking you up with my dick in about an hour."

I laughed as I closed my eyes. He was adorable, sexy, funny, and ambitious. Good thing I was leaving in two days. I could get used to having him in my bed.

Chapter Nineteen

Taylor

I lay awake long after Livi's breathing evened out, signaling that she was asleep. Man, her ex was a fucking moron. Sex with her had been...different. Good different. No, amazing different. Don't hate on me, but I knew I was spectacular in bed. I knew how to make girls say my name. Hearing Livi *scream* my name like she did? My whole body reacted. I couldn't have stopped my release if I had wanted to. Plus, I didn't pull out. I'd never done that before. I didn't trust condoms, ninety-eight percent effective wasn't effective enough for my liking. But with her, I didn't want to. Like some weird primal instinct took over and I wanted to feel like I was shooting off inside her.

I had been losing my mind from the moment that girl had walked into my life. Thank god I'd finally fucked her. Now my mind would stop going places it had no business going, and my body would stop reacting to the mere sound of her voice. I was ready to get back to my normal awesome self.

I closed my eyes, wrapped my arms tighter around Livi and fell asleep.

***

My eyes opened when I heard birds chirping. The sun was shining and the sky was cloudless. I looked down at Livi. I was literally wrapped around her body like fucking ivy. What the hell? I did it again. I'd spooned her all night.

Carefully, I untwined my body from hers. She was still naked. Lightly, I trailed my fingertips down the middle of her body, from throat to belly button. I brought my fingers back up, circling her breasts in turn. I stopped at the right one and rolled her nipple between my finger and thumb.

I grinned when I saw her smile.

"Good morning, Taylor. Is there something I can do for you?"

"Why yes, Livi. As a matter of fact, if you could get on all fours and stick your tight little ass in the air, that would be lovely." To my delight, she did exactly as I'd requested. "That's my girl."

Oh shit. Did I say that out loud?

Livi looked over her shoulder at me. "Well?"

I smirked, grateful that she didn't hear my slip or didn't care enough to comment on it. "Impatient much?"

She raised an eyebrow. "You woke me up from a dead sleep, asked me to bend over, and you call me impatient?"

"You're right. I apologize." I moved behind her, kneeling. I ran my fingers down her ass before dipping them into her core to make sure she was ready for me. She was so fucking wet, I couldn't believe it. I grabbed a condom and put it on before positioning the head of my dick against her pussy. "Tell me if this doesn't feel good."

I could hear the teasing in her voice. "Believe me you'll be the first to know."

I shook my head. "Such a smart-ass in the mornings. I'll have to remember that." I needed to shut my mouth. There was no reason to remember her morning temperament. She was a fling, not my future wife. I placed my hands on her ass, easing into her and trying to clear any and all emotion out of my brain.

I buried myself balls deep and then ground against her.

"Oh god…"

"Yes?"

I felt her laughter, making her pussy tighten even more around my cock. Grinning, I pulled out and then sank back in slowly, grinding against her. I repeated this over and over and over. I could tell when she started getting close to the edge. Every time I started to pull out, she would follow me, not wanting me to leave her body.

"Harder, Taylor."

I gripped her hips and slammed into her once. "Like that?"

"Oh god, yes. Don't stop. Please don't stop."

I slid out, using her hips for leverage I pulled her body toward me as I drove in again. And again. She felt so good, too good. I was close. Another "Oh Taylor" out of her and I wasn't going to make it. I reached up with one hand, gently fisting my fingers in her hair, tugging lightly, the way I'd learned she liked.

"Come for me, sugar." I pounded into her over and over, not stopping, not caring about the sounds the bed was making as it moved across the floor.

"Oh god, oh god, Taylor. Holy. Fuck."

I felt her body clench around my dick seconds before I came. We both collapsed on the mattress at the same time. I should care that I was lying on top of her, but I didn't feel like leaving her body. Ever.

Chapter Twenty

Livi

A few minutes after we came down, Taylor rolled off me and I took a big deep breath. I could have told him that he was making it hard for me to breathe, but being covered by his body had felt nice. Safe almost, like one of those weighted blankets that people liked to sleep under.

Knock. Knock. Knock.

"Hey, Liv? Wait. Why is this door locked? Are you awake?"

Instantly, I sat up and looked at Taylor. Instead of appearing panicked, like I was sure I did, he looked smug and cocky. I shook my head, smiling as I whispered, "Get out of here before Bailey breaks the door down."

"Nah. Tell her to leave." To prove his point he crawled up my body, forcing me back against the bed. He leaned down, taking my nipple into his mouth, biting it lightly.

"Uh, yeah, I'm awake. I'm, um, changing." I clamped my lips together, trying to keep from moaning. Taylor's mouth was still at my breast, but his hands were moving much farther south.

"Why did you lock the door? We've all seen you naked."

Taylor moved his mouth to my ear, speaking softly. "Mmmm, yes we have." He took my earlobe in his teeth.

"Bailey. I'll be out in a second."

"Hurry. Everyone is super hungover. I need you to make that smoothie thing."

"Okay." I slapped Taylor's ass when I heard her walk away. "You are impossible."

He grabbed my hand and brought it between us, placing it on his rigid cock. "I'm insatiable too."

"Again? Already?" I raised my eyebrows.

"You make me feel like a horny teenager." He winked.

I pushed against his chest, trying to get him to let me up. "Sorry. Bailey will be back here in like two minutes. She has the patience of a small child when she's hungover."

"Come on, sugar, please... It'll take me no time at all."

I snorted. "Oh, lucky me."

Taylor stood up on his knees and pointed to his rigid dick. "What am I supposed to do with this? I can't walk into the house with a raging boner."

My resolve wavered. Surely we had time for one more round before Bailey started yelling. I'd need to be quieter, obviously, but there was no need to waste a perfectly good hard-on.

Now who was acting like a horny teenager?

I glanced over on the bedside table. "Where are the rest of the condoms?"

Taylor scrubbed his hands down his face, wincing. "Uh, they are in the bathroom in the bunk room."

I shrugged apologetically. "Looks like you are going to be walking into the house with a pillow in front of your cock." I climbed off the bed and started digging around in my bag for something to wear.

Taylor flung himself down dramatically, throwing his arm over his eyes. "Unless we don't use one."

I popped up. "What?"

He rolled over to face me, grinning. "Never have I ever had sex without a condom before."

I wasn't sure I could believe him. I supposed it was possible. Players like Taylor were always careful, that much I remembered from my single days. Part of me wanted to agree with what he was proposing. For some reason my body was craving that depth of intimacy with the tan Georgian god pouting in my bed.

I had been disgusted when I found out Patrick had been cheating. The next day I went and got tested for every disease I could possibly think of. Thankfully, my doctor's office called with the test results and assured me I was clean.

I was on birth control, but sex without a condom with the guy I'd met two days ago still didn't seem like the responsible thing to do.

Before I could answer him Taylor started to laugh. "Calm down, sugar. I can see your wheels turning. I was kidding."

I got up and grabbed a tank top, a pair of cutoff shorts, and his ball cap from the nightstand. He licked his lips, his hands snaking out to grab me as I threaded my ponytail through his hat. I smirked at him before stepping out of his reach and headed into the house.

Chapter Twenty-One

Taylor

What in the holy hell had come out of my mouth? I'd asked her if I could fuck her without a condom. I would love to say that I actually *had* been kidding. I would love to say that I was *that* horny, that desperate to get back inside her. I'm afraid that neither was the case. I had liked the idea of not wearing one with her. The idea of it turned me on beyond belief. I pulled on my shorts after she left and went out the side door in search of a cold shower and a lobotomy.

After I dressed for the day and mentally beat the shit out of myself, I wandered into the kitchen. Livi was standing at the counter, looking gorgeous as hell in my ball cap, pouring a pitcher of smoothies into plastic cups.

I leaned over her shoulder, peering inside the blender. "What's that?"

She used her perfectly tight ass to push me back, glancing nervously in the direction of the table where everyone was sitting.

I snorted. "Sugar, if you comin' out of your room wearing my hat doesn't make your friends suspicious, then me touching your shoulder isn't going to either."

"Hangover cure." She ignored my statement and decided to talk about what was in the blender instead. "Seems after we went to bed, those guys all kept drinking."

I leaned in to whisper in her ear, "After *we* went to bed?"

Her body tensed when she realized what she had said. No one had caught it though. They were all hurting that bad. I grabbed the tray of cups and brought it to the table, passing them around for her.

I took a sip of Cole's before handing it to him. "What's in this? It tastes like shit."

Cole snorted. "Tell us, Tay, what exactly does shit taste like?"

I got down next to Cole's ear and yelled, "YOU MAKE THE LAMEST JOKES WHEN YOU ARE HUNGOVER." I smirked when he grabbed his head in pain. I patted his back. "Drink your shit smoothie, buddy."

Livi came and sat down next to Kasey, pulling her in for a hug. I was jealous. I wanted a hug. "It does not taste like shit. It tastes healthy. It's full of fruit, B twelve drops, electrolytes, and beer. It hydrates you and gives you a little hair of the dog." She stroked Kasey's hair. "You guys will feel better in no time."

Bailey slammed her smoothie like it was an Irish Car Bomb. She pulled out her phone and handed it to Livi. "Patrick called me this morning looking for you. He said you weren't answering your phone."

Livi paled, her eyes going impossibly wide. "Oh, uh, weird. I didn't have a missed call from him. I'll call him back later."

"Call him now." Bailey sat her phone down on the table in front of Livi. "He seemed really worried about you.

I must have had a weird look on my face because Cole kicked me under the table. I got up and walked outside. For some reason I couldn't stomach the thought of having to listen to Livi pretend to be married to keep her friends in the dark.

Why the hell was her ex calling her anyway? And also, why in the flying fuck was any of it bothering me as much as it was?

I turned when the screen door squeaked open and Livi came out carrying Bailey's cell in one hand and a cup of coffee in the other. She sat in a chair and put the phone down beside her, pulling her legs underneath her. I leaned my back against the railing, arms folded across my chest. "You going to call him?"

She looked up at me, defeated. "No. He knows I haven't told them about the divorce. He's being an ass. Bailey wouldn't let up though."

"She's protective about you."

Livi shrugged. "She knows something's up. She's trying to get it out of me." She looked so sad all of a sudden. The playful, sexy girl I had been with all morning had left the moment her ex-husband had been brought up. I wanted to beat the shit out of her ex. I wanted Bailey to leave Livi alone. I wanted to have my happy Livi back.

"Let's get out of here."

She brightened instantly, which I took as a hella good sign. "Where are we going? What if everyone wants to come with us?"

I chuckled, shaking my head. "Where we're going, sugar, they won't want to follow."

I held out my hand, needing to touch her. She took it, and for some reason I didn't want to think about too closely, my heart did a little kick flip in my chest. As soon as we turned the corner to the kitchen Livi dropped my hand like I had burned her. I looked up and saw Bailey staring at us from across the room. Damn, did that woman ever mind her own fucking business?

"So Liv and I were talking about heading out for a jog around the lake. Anyone want to join us?" I grinned as everyone at the table let out a collective groan. "Hmmmm, I'll take that as a *no thank you*? Too bad. It feels great out there this morning." I turned, rather pleased with my brilliant self, and went to put on my running shoes when motherf'in Bailey spoke up.

"I'm not down for the jog but I'll drive over to the other side of the lake and meet y'all at the beach entrance from yesterday. That sound okay?"

No. That most certainly did not sound okay. That sounded like I wasn't going to get to spread Livi out naked and wet on a towel and have my way with her. I plastered a smile on my face, because what else could I do?

"Of course. Why don't you see if you can rally the rest of the troops and we'll meet you guys at the beach entrance in about forty-five minutes?"

"Do you really think it'll take y'all that long? We hiked over there yesterday and it only took us thirty."

Was Bailey put on this earth to ruin my damn life? Jesus with this chick. "We're going to go a longer way. It's an easier path to run." I made sure my next words were clear. "We'll. Meet. You. There." I turned on my heels and went to change clothes.

Only problem was, I started to follow Livi to her room, where my clothes were, where my clothes were not allowed to be. Of course, Bailey the detective noticed. "Why are you going to Livi's room?"

I stopped and spun around, making sure I put some confusion in my eyes. "Uh. I have no idea. It's early. I'm still fuzzy."

Quickly, I went into the bunk room I was supposed to be sharing with Cole. How the hell was I going to pull this off? I had clearly been thinking solely with my dick when I put *all* my clothes under Livi's bed. I smiled to myself thinking of that bed. The noises I had gotten that girl to make. The way her tight—

Tap. Tap. Tap.

I walked across the room to the window and laughed at what I saw. Livi was standing outside holding some clothes and my tennis shoes. I opened the window, taking the pile from her hands. "Thank you, sugar." I winked and went to change.

My brain wasn't working. Thank goodness hers was.

Chapter Twenty-Two

Livi

I jogged beside Taylor, silently trying my best to keep my thoughts in the here and now and not think about Bailey uncovering the truth, or what the hell Patrick was doing using my friends to get ahold of me. As if reading my mind, Taylor stopped and leaned against a tree, sweat pouring down his chiseled abs.

"Sugar, you're thinking so hard you're hurting *my* head."

I sat down on a stump, taking a swig from the water bottle in my hand. "I know. I'm sorry. I'll stop."

Tay came over and kneeled in front of me, barely panting. "Livi, you don't have to apologize. You have a lot going on right now. I hate to see that sad look on your face, though. It breaks my heart."

"Since when do you, the self-proclaimed selfish bastard, have a heart?" My smile faded when I saw a panicked look wash over his flushed face. "Tay? I was kidding. I don't think you are selfish, or a bastard."

All at once he fused his mouth to mine, his tongue dancing. I may have moaned. I'm not ashamed, he was gorgeous and shirtless, and making my toes curl. I put my arms around his neck as he picked me up. He had me up against a huge pine tree, my legs wrapped around his waist. I could feel his hard cock against my core. We were a mess of hands and mouths, fumbling to remove clothes, desperate to touch. Taylor put me back down only long enough to rip off my shorts and tear my panties.

"Tay. If you ask me, I'll take them off, you don't have to rip them."

He gave me that devilish grin of his. "You love it when I rip them." He kissed my neck. "You love knowing how much I want you. How impatient I am to be inside you."

"Yes, I do. I love it. But I'm on vacation. I only brought so many pairs."

"I'll send you some replacements when I get home." He winked as he rolled on a condom.

"You brought condoms on our jog?"

"You said you didn't want to have sex without one. So yeah, of course, I brought condoms on our jog."

He picked me back up, like I weighed next to nothing, and entered me in one fluid motion. My god he was the sexiest, smoothest man I had ever been with. He made me feel wanton and uninhibited. We were fucking against a tree off a well-worn path. Anyone could come by. We could be caught at any second, but no part of me cared. Taylor put his hand behind my back, making sure the tree bark didn't scrape my exposed skin. He set a deliciously decadent pace, thrusting up into me in a punishing rhythm. Obviously he didn't care if we were caught either.

"Oh god, Taylor. So. Good. Please. Don't. Stop." Each word was punctuated with the feel of him hitting the most amazing spot inside me.

He laughed against my neck, sending chills down my spine. "Sugar, that's one thing you'll never have to worry about. I won't ever stop before you're done. I won't ever stop until I feel you shatter around me."

I leaned my head against the tree, closing my eyes, letting everything go. The only thing in my world right now was Taylor. Taylor and the mind-blowing orgasm that was building inside me. His teeth grazed my collarbone, his lips kissed my neck, his tongue flicked my earlobe. I came instantly and seconds later I felt him follow. He set me down and leaned his forehead again mine.

Out of breath, he panted, "This is the best jog I have ever been on. Ever."

I laughed and we got dressed, drank some water, and headed out on the path again.

After tappin' it against a tree we were both moving slow. Neither one of us felt the urge to jog anymore. By the time we made it to the beach entrance of the lake it had taken closer to an hour. I could see everyone in the water, everyone except Bailey. She was on the beach, her phone to her ear.

I stopped short and put my arm out to halt Taylor. "Let's turn around and hide in the woods for the rest of the weekend."

Taylor threw his arm around my neck, kissing my head. "I would love nothing more than to run away with you. But we both know that your friend Bailey would promptly launch a well-organized search party. We'd be found by nightfall."

I snorted and started walking toward the sounds of laughter and splashing water. Taylor stripped off his shirt and dove into the lake as soon as it was deep enough. He turned and winked at me as he surfaced and swam farther out to meet Cole.

I could feel Bailey's eyes on my back, trying to burn a hole straight through me like she could see inside my heart to figure out what was going on. I took a deep breath and spun around to face her, a smile firmly in place.

"Bailey, you swimming today?" I peeled off my sweat-soaked shirt and kicked off my shoes.

She crossed her arms over her ample chest and cocked out one hip. "Livi, we need to talk." She looked like a pissed-off sassy teenager, which was on point since she actually had no real idea what was happening around her.

I took off my socks and then went to pull down my shorts. I froze instantly when I remembered I was no longer wearing anything underneath them. Crap, stupid Taylor, sexy panty ripper. "Okay, but hurry. It's hot as hell and I'm sweating like a whore in church." I bit my lips together to keep from laughing at my own joke. I mean, I had sex against a tree thirty minutes ago.

"Patrick called again, he said you never returned his call. What's going on? Is this about Taylor? Is there something going on between you two?"

I sighed and hung my head. Own up to my failed marriage before I was ready or tell partial truths? Easy way out sounded really good right now. "Patrick and I got into a big fight before I left for this trip." There, that wasn't a lie at all. "I told him I needed some space, to clear my head. I asked him not to call me."

I had asked the prick not to call me, but that was months ago through my lawyer.

She looked at the ground, kicking at some rocks. "What was the fight about?"

I shrugged her question off, like it was no big deal. "Stupid married people stuff, you know how it goes." She'd been with her husband a year longer than I'd been with Patrick. Dumb fights were part of the deal when you spent your life with someone.

Bailey put one hand up to shield her eyes from the bright afternoon sun, peering out to our friends laughing in the lake. "What about Taylor?"

I narrowed my eyes. "What about him, Bailey?"

"Is there something going on between you two? I've seen y'all, You're attached at the hip." Her eyes studied my exposed skin, like she was searching for clues. Maybe she'd find some.

"He makes me laugh. We have fun together. I'm not being unfaithful, Bailey, I promise." None of that was a lie either. I could spout half-truths all damn day. "Now stop worrying about me and come have some fun."

I walked into the bacteria-ridden water wearing my sports bra and shorts with Bailey right beside me.

Chapter Twenty-Three

Taylor

I beamed when I spotted Livi finally swimming toward me. I had seen the stress etched on her face when she was talking to Bailey on the shore. I wanted to reach for her hand and drag her to me. I wanted to kiss her temple to make her smile, and pinch her ass to make her laugh. I wanted, uh, to know where the hell my balls had gone.

Two nights wrapped around Livi and I sounded like a sentimental douche.

Cole sent a wave of water into my face, breaking my inner monologue. "All right, ladies, what is the game plan for the rest of the day? The night? Y'all still want to head into town and go to the bar?"

Allie was floating on her back, sporting some oversize black shades that made her look like a dead president's wife. I thought she was asleep until she answered Cole slowly. "I say we spend the rest of the day being lazy. Then we shower and head out for a night on the town. I wanna dance with an old cowboy."

I chuckled. "An old cowboy? What's the difference?"

Kasey cocked her head. "What's the difference? How about everything. Livi, you have a way with words. Why don't you describe it for them?"

Livi pursed her perfect lips, like she was trying to think of the right thing to say to make a silly boy like me understand. "That is an impossible thing to put into words."

I reached under the water and ran my hand up her inner thigh. I loved the way chill bumps broke out on her arms and a smile danced in her green eyes. "Try."

She sighed, tapping her chin. "When you dance with an old cowboy, there is never any rush. You feel it in the way they hold you, steady and respectful. They want nothing from you, other than your company for a song or two. They take care of you for the short time that you belong to them. They have an unwavering rhythm. The way they dance is so ingrained in who they are, there is never a missed step. It's peaceful and calm. For those three minutes, nothing else matters except for the nice man holding your hand."

I wanted to be that man. I wanted to make Livi's world perfect, even if it was only for a few minutes. Obviously, I couldn't say any of those things out loud. It terrified me that I was even thinking them. I couldn't tell her that I was silently praying that I danced like an old cowboy.

So instead I said, "You know I've been told a time or two that I have an unrelenting rhythm."

Livi rolled her eyes and slapped my arm. "I said unwavering, you jackass."

Cole puckered his lips, thinking. "Do you have to be old to dance like an old cowboy?"

Allie, still floating, answered. "Of course not. It's in the *way* you dance. Not your age." That woman was like a piece of Styrofoam; she seemed like she could float from here to Florida.

I tuned the rest of the conversation out when it turned to the Disney channel and some kind of dancing man show. I sank down in the water to my shoulders and reached out for Livi's hand. She smiled without looking in my direction, making sure it didn't give us away to the rest of the group.

My brain was going a mile a minute. What the hell was my deal? I'd had her. I got what I needed, a few times now. So why was I still so bent out of shape over this girl? Okay, so maybe she *was* gorgeous and sexy and smart and funny and adventurous and compassionate. Plus, she wrote fucking porn for a living. But still, she was only a girl here for a weekend. Yet here I was, wanting to hold her hand, and to dance with her like an old cowboy.

Kasey put her palms on Allie's stomach and pushed her under water. "That's enough. It's unnatural how well you float. Let's head home, I want to take a nap."

Allie came up looking like a drowned cat, big black shades and all. "You are so lucky I am too hungover to make any sudden movements."

As those two started heading back to shore, Bailey turned to Livi. "You going to jog home too?"

My heart did a small victory dance when Livi looked to me for the answer. It meant she was with me, jog or no jog. "That's up to you, sugar."

Livi shook her head at my continued use of her pet name in front of her friends. By this point, I didn't even realize I was doing it. "Let's ride back with everyone else. I want to have enough time to lie down before I need to shower." She pulled her hand out of mine and grabbed my dick. Oh, by lie down she meant fuck.

Nice. Me too.

***

When we got back to the house, Bailey tried to ruin my life yet again. "Liv, why don't you come and nap inside. It's so much cooler in here."

I must have accidentally growled out loud because Cole came up and patted me on the back. I guess he thought I was choking on air.

"Uh. I, uh, don't want to lie on the couch. I'm all wet."

I really did choke that time, but Cole didn't bother to come to my rescue a second time. He was also one of those people who only said bless you once. If you were going to keep sneezing, you were on your own with the devil.

"There isn't enough room for me in y'alls beds."

I held my hand in the air. "You know, Livi, you can always share my bed if you want to stay inside."

Bailey put her hands on her hips, shooting daggers into my skull with her eyes. "She's. Married." The venom in her tone was impressive.

I snorted. "Does that mean she isn't allowed to nap in the air conditioning?"

Baily narrowed her eyes even further, which I didn't really think was possible until I saw it happen myself. "It means she can't share a bed with another man. Ass."

Liv dropped her head. I couldn't tell if she was irritated with me or with Bailey. "I am fine on my nice little porch bed. Thank you, *all*, for the concern. Bailey, honey, please stop reminding me that I am married." She slammed the door and I heard her throw the lock in place.

Oops. Oh well, I was planning on using the side entrance anyway.

Chapter Twenty-Four

Livi

I peeled off my wet clothes and slipped on a t-shirt and shorts before flopping down on the unmade bed. I was starting to get a headache. Bailey was eventually going to cause a scene, and Taylor seemed like he would never back down when it came to wanting me. Perfect.

Tonight, we'd be drinking. Sure as I was lying here, I'd let Taylor hold me and touch me and Bailey would lose her shit. She'd climb on her moral high horse and start preaching about the sanctity of marriage.

Patrick was never a stellar husband. Bailey knew this, but for some reason she was hell-bent on making sure I toed the line this weekend. I knew she was trying to be a good friend, and I loved her for it, but it was also starting to cap my house.

I heard the side door open and couldn't stop my smile. "Must you antagonize her?"

Taylor sighed and crawled into bed. "Yep. I must." He rolled on top of me, not doing anything to shield me from his full weight. He kissed the tip of my nose. "I'm sorry. I'll try to be better with her, I promise. I don't want to stress you out, but I want her to mind her own business."

I laughed humorlessly. "To Bailey, everything is her business."

Taylor kissed his way down my neck and nibbled on my collarbone. "Yeah? Well guess what? *We* aren't her business. We are two single adults, willing and able to have an amazing weekend fling. On Sunday, when you tell them the truth, she'll realize that."

I nodded. "Right. Sunday. When I tell my friends all about my failed marriage, and my weekend fling drives one direction while I fly in the other. Can we skip Sunday? Can I go right to Monday instead?"

He smiled against my neck where he was raining kisses again. "Why Monday? Don't people usually hate Mondays?"

I leaned my head back and closed my eyes. "I work from home. Mondays don't bother me all that much. Monday is when my life goes back to normal and I don't have to explain anything to anybody. All I have to do is unpack and do laundry. Maybe write a few sex scenes." I said the last part to torture him.

Taylor rolled us over, settling me on top of him. "But, my little literary porn star, there is no me on Monday. Doesn't that make you a little sad?"

I rubbed my hands down his muscular chest, scraping his flesh lightly with my nails. "The truth?"

He nodded. "Yes, please."

I flicked his nipple, punishing him for making this moment too serious. "I know I'm supposed to keep emotions out of it, but I'll miss you when I leave. I'm not going to cry for days or anything." I grinned and flicked his other nipple. "But I'll be bummed."

He sat up, cupping my face in his hands. For once, his eyes held no humor, no laughter. "You are the most amazing woman I have ever met. Ever. I'll be bummed too."

I ran my tongue along his lower lip, satisfied when I heard him groan. I didn't want to talk about Sunday. I didn't want to admit I genuinely liked him and that I would most likely tear up when we said good-bye.

Taylor was funny, charming, smart, and sexy as hell. He made me feel wanted. He made me feel special. I would without a doubt feel his absence in my heart. I hadn't meant to let him in, but somewhere between spooning and letting him fuck me against a tree, I had.

Taylor rolled me back over, pinning my hands above my head, and within seconds he had us both naked.

"You in a hurry?"

He answered with his mouth around my nipple. "Ah-huh. I want to make you scream so loud I have to cover your mouth so your friends don't hear. Then I want to take a nap."

My laughter was cut off by the sensation of him entering me slowly and to the hilt. "Mmmm, sounds perfect."

Usually Taylor was everywhere, his mouth and hands a blur of pleasure. His body taking mine hard and unyielding. This time it was like everything was happening in slow motion. He flowed in and out of my body at a tantalizing pace.

"Oh wow. Oh Taylor."

His mouth was at my ear. "Do you like it like this too, sugar?"

I nodded. I couldn't seem to find my voice. Every time he would bury himself inside me, he would grind his hips against mine. Every grind brought me closer and closer to the edge. I knew my moans and whimpers were getting too loud. I was giving him everything he wanted. He molded his mouth to mine, absorbing my cries as I came.

I felt him pull away slightly.

"Look at me, Livi."

I opened my eyes and watched him fall apart.

Chapter Twenty-Five

Taylor

Holy mother fuck. I was staring up at the ceiling while Liv slept nestled against my side. Any other girl and I would have been contemplating how I could slip out of the bed without waking her. With Livi, I was contemplating how for the first time in my life I had made love to a woman. I've fucked, banged, nailed, screwed, boned, and laid. A lot. But never have I ever, until now, made love.

I couldn't tell her with words how I felt about her. She would have either run for the hills or laughed in my face. So instead I showed her how much she meant to me. I even wanted to look into her eyes as I came. Could I be any more of a pussy? I submit that I cannot.

I sighed as I pulled Livi closer to me, finally drifting off to sleep.

***

I woke up alone. Damn it all to hell. I was unhappy about it. I left out the side door in search of people. The house was a flurry of activity and noise. There were blow dryers running, music blaring, and girls going from one room to the next. I walked into "my room" and found Cole lying on the bottom bunk, his hands behind his head.

"Hey, man, are you hiding? Good call. Breathing in that many aerosol fumes has got to be a health hazard."

Cole snorted and reached for a cup on the nightstand. "Yeah, there was too much estrogen in there. They are all getting ready in the same bathroom. Makes absolutely no fucking sense."

I went and sat next to him on the bed, stealing his drink.

"Jack already? The sun has barely set."

"It seemed appropriate to start drinking early. Bailey and Livi kind of got into it for a few minutes. I hate it when people argue. I'm from a broken home, you know." He took his drink back.

Broken home, shmoken home. Cole's parents got divorced *last* year. "Yes, you poor emotionally stunted little boy. What were they fighting about?"

"What do you think?" He handed me back the Jack and Coke.

I took a long swallow. "Global warming?"

"Ehhhaaaa." He made the universal incorrect buzzer noise. "Bailey asked Livi if she called her husband—"

I felt compelled to interrupt with, "*Ex*-husband."

Cole ignored my interjection completely and continued talking. "Livi told her that she hadn't and that she wasn't planning on it and that Bailey should drop it. Bailey got all bitchy and told Livi she needed to wake up and realize that she was making terrible choices this weekend. Livi told her to shut it. Then Allie turned the radio up and started singing obnoxiously loud."

I let out a sigh and lay back on the bed beside my best friend. "So Bailey thinks that Livi is cheating on her husband and I'm the big bad wolf who's making her do it."

"It's not like you are being subtle, either one of you. You are constantly looking at Liv like you are five seconds away from mounting her, and she stares at you like you're both savior and sin."

I scrubbed my hands down my face. "Ugh, I know. But I can't seem to help myself around Livi. I want her. Like all the damn time. You want to know the worst part?"

"Of course."

"It's not only that I want to hump her in every room of this house. I want to hold her hand and rub her back and kiss her forehead. Ya know, to be sweet. You were right last night, I like her. Like, *like her* like her." Cole's eyes widened in surprise at my confession. I couldn't blame him. All of this was one hundred percent out of character for me.

He reached over and slapped my cheek, hard and without warning. "Snap out of it right this goddamn second. You are Taylor Hill. You don't *like* girls. You fuck girls. I told you at the beginning of this trip, *she isn't for you.* Now get your head on straight and be the arrogant asshole I know you can be. Acting like you want more will only hurt her in the end. We both know commitment is NOT your thing."

Commitment wasn't my thing. Well, neither was spooning, or fucking without protection, or making love, or any of the other crazy things I'd wanted since meeting Livi. But I knew deep down that Cole was right. The best thing for Livi in the long run was for me to be the old Taylor. The one who only wanted sex and wouldn't care enough to try to make her smile or laugh. Wouldn't put in the effort to try to make her feel special. The old Taylor was a dick. For once in my life, the thought of being the old me made me want to puke.

I looked up when Allie stuck her head in the door. She was wearing the smallest dress I had ever seen and a pair of well-worn cowboy boots. "Hey, boys." Allie had a smile that could melt a glacier. "Would y'all mind making us some drinks?"

Cole stood and made his way across the room. "Tay needs to hop in the shower, but I would be more than happy to help you lovely ladies with your pre-game."

Allie gave a little smirk. "Y'alls' pregame too."

I stood heading for the bathroom. "We can't pregame, y'all hired us to drive your drunk asses around."

"Bailey hired a driver." Allie turned and headed back into the living room.

Cole grabbed her arm and halted her forward motion. "What do you mean Bailey hired a driver? She hired *us*. To drive you."

"It's Bailey. Who knows why she does anything? She said that it was our last night and we all needed some fun. So she called the local cab company and paid them out the ass to have someone drive us all in the Suburban."

Cole let go of Allie and spared a glance in my direction, eyebrows raised in question. I shrugged, as confused as Cole was. I said, "Well, either Bailey really wants to have some fun tonight, or she's plotting my murder and she wants me to be too drunk to fend her off."

Allie laughed all the way to the kitchen.

Cole shook his head, a serious look on his face. "Don't joke, man. I could easily see Bailey knowing how to pull off the perfect murder."

Chapter Twenty-Six

Livi

Bailey had been hot and cold all evening. She gave me shit, once again, about not calling Patrick back, and for flirting with Taylor. It was almost comical. If she had any idea about half the things I'd actually done with Taylor this weekend, she'd have a heart attack. Prim and proper Bailey, always the voice of reason. Then, out of nowhere, she had flipped a one eighty and hired a driver so the guys could party with us.

I sipped my drink, staring at myself in the reflection of the patio door. I was about to be a thirty-year-old divorced woman. My weekend fling with Taylor had done wonders for my self-esteem though. He made me feel sexy. He made me *feel*, period. How the hell was I going to walk away from him? How was I supposed to let him go? Even though I tried to push the thoughts away and deny they were there, I was falling for him. For every damn thing about him.

I'd learned nothing. After all these years, and one divorce later, I was still the girl falling for the wrong guy. I had dated (and I use that term loosely) so many wrong guys in college. The eternal partier, the mildly abusive asshole, the coke addict, the frat boy, the commitment-phobe... I mean the list could go on for pages. Then I'd married a man I had thought was the right guy. Maybe he was at first, then he turned into another wrong one, way wrong.

Taylor was a gorgeous playboy who would break my heart come Sunday morning. Some fools never learn, I suppose.

Kasey walked up and put her chin on my shoulder, staring at our reflection in the glass. "How you doin', Livi Lou?"

I rested my cheek against her head. "I'm great. I've had an amazing weekend, and now I get to go out and dance and drink with my girls." I lowered my voice considerably before adding, "Then I get to come home and have utterly mind-blowing sex with a man Bailey hired."

Kasey snorted. "So you *are* nailing the help?"

"Yes. Did you have any doubt?"

"Not really. I like Taylor. I like you and Taylor. He makes you smile, and the way he looks at you from across the room, hell, it even turns me on."

I huffed out a little laugh. "It's a weekend fling, Kasey. Don't read too much into it. Come tomorrow I'll be flying home to write make-believe love stories and he'll be off making someone else, uh, smile." Kasey and I both turned and watched as Taylor entered the room. He looked hot as hell. He was wearing gray shorts, a white button-down with the sleeves rolled up, and black Converse. The white shirt made his summer tan look even darker. His gaze immediately found me. He flashed that adorable cocky grin of his and headed right for us.

Kasey hummed quietly, "Will he though?"

Taylor slid his arm around my waist and quickly kissed my temple before stepping away. "Will he what?"

I opened my mouth to change the subject, but Kasey spoke before I had the chance. "Will you be off tomorrow looking for the next girl to fall into bed with?"

Taylor's smile never faltered as he answered her, "No. Tomorrow I will be nursing a broken heart." He winked at me, making *my* heart skip a beat.

Kasey nodded. "Good answer, son."

Taylor saluted her with his beer bottle before asking, "What's the deal with Bailey hiring a driver? I thought that was why she hired Cole and me?"

"Who the hell knows? I figured she was feeling a little guilty for giving you and Liv such a hard time all weekend. That's Bail's M.O. Get all pissy and blow her lid, then apologize by doing something over-the-top nice." Kasey gestured to me. "Am I right?"

"Sounds about right to me." I gave Taylor an evil grin. "Or maybe she wants to kill you and thought it'd be easier if you were wasted?"

Taylor's smirk disappeared. "No joke, I said those exact words to Cole like five minutes ago."

I leaned my head against his shoulder. "Aw, Tay, don't worry. I'll protect you from Bailey."

Before he could say anything else, Allie climbed up on the table. That poor table had taken a pounding from us this weekend. "All right, if everyone could grab a shot and gather around, I want to make a toast." Once we had all done as we were told she continued, "First of all, thank you, Bailey, for once again planning an amazing trip for us, and for hiring these adorable guys to make our drinks and make us laugh. That being said, on our last night I hope we *all* go so hard."

We took our shots, vodka, typical Allie.

Bailey turned to Taylor and my breath hitched. Was she going to bitch him out about his flirting, and threaten to call his boss? "Taylor, I want to apologize for giving you such a hard time all weekend. I want what's best for Livi and—"

"I know you do." Taylor held up his hands, placatingly. "Believe me, so do I. So you will be happy to know, I was a good boy all weekend."

Kasey hid her giggles behind Cole's shoulder and Cole choked on his whiskey. Allie looked equal parts confused and excited. Me, I was praying Bailey didn't get what Taylor was actually saying.

Bailey's eyebrows raised in question as she turned her attention on me. "Really?"

Taylor placed his hand on my shoulder and collarbone, giving it an affectionate squeeze. "Tell her, sugar, tell Bailey how good I've been."

I bit the inside of my cheek to keep from smiling, which was something I would've done in high school knowing it was inappropriate and doing it anyway. Nonetheless, I nodded quickly. "He has been so good. Mind-blowing."

Cole choked again. Before this weekend was over that guy was going to need CPR. Kasey hid her whole body behind him and Allie wrinkled her nose, apparently still not sure what was happening. Bailey smiled like she was utterly relieved. "That's so great, I'm sorry for doubting you guys." She looked down when her phone dinged and then told us our driver was here.

We all filed outside and climbed in the car. Cole and Taylor in the third row, Allie, Kasey, and I in the middle, and of course Bailey in the front giving the Georgia native directions to a bar that was seven minutes away.

Taylor put his hand on the back of my neck, holding me in place while he whispered in my ear. "Mind-blowing, huh?"

His breath in my ear sent shivers up my spine. In that instant all I wanted to do was climb into his lap and ride him the whole way to the bar. Taylor made me feel like the women I write about. Completely and wholly infatuated with a guy. Lust and love. I turned in my seat; I knew my expression was full of desire, I couldn't help it. "Mind-blowing."

His face was inches away from mine and I witnessed the moment his eyes went from playful to aroused.

I smiled. "In fact, it's all I can think about."

He moved his mouth to my ear once again. "Say the word, baby, and I will pull you back here with me." He nuzzled my neck, breathing me in. "Mmmm, you smell edible. Please say the word, sugar."

Cole moved his face next to ours and obnoxiously cleared his throat, shattering the moment. "Could you guys please try to control yourselves? My god, you just got away with telling Bailey you've been fucking all weekend without her even realizing it. Now stop touching until we get to the damn bar. I want to be well and wasted before realization dawns on her and she loses her shit."

Chapter Twenty-Seven

Taylor

The bar was small, even by old honky-tonk standards. There was a band set up in one corner playing classic country songs, and playing them well. I still had a semi from the car ride over. I wanted to grab Livi's hand and lead her to the nearest bathroom stall. Not romantic, I know, but damn I wanted to be inside that girl. It didn't help that she looked like sex on a stick. She had on another pair of cutoff shorts, a loose tank top, and brown boots. You knew that she wasn't even trying to look fuckable, she simply *was*. The girls went in search of a table while Cole and I headed to the bar. We figured since Bailey had essentially given us the night off, we could cover the bar tab. How much could the four of them drink anyway?

We brought a round of beers and shots to the table. The song that played was fast and up-tempo, I could see Cole fidgeting in his seat. He loved to dance, although he'd never admit it out loud.

I put my hand on Livi's thigh. "Sugar, dance with Cole for me. He's going to wiggle out of his damn chair."

She laughed and then stood and grabbed Cole's hand. "Dance with me, C."

I loved hearing her call my best friend by my nickname for him. It was that same weird domestic feeling that had washed over me when we were cooking the girls' dinner on night one.

They got up and Cole took Livi's other hand and walked her to the little dance floor. Watching him expertly twirl, spin, and push her around the floor only made that feeling grow. Normally, if Cole was dancing with a chick I was planning on nailing after we were done barhopping, I'd get irritated. It'd mean more work for me if he was nicer than I was, which was usually the case. Right now, watching two of my favorite people laugh and dance together made me feel content. I was turning into a sappy bastard. The song ended and a slow one began as Cole brought Livi back to me.

I stood, taking her hand and pulling her onto the dance floor and into my arms. "Does Cole dance like an old cowboy?"

She snorted. "Cole dances like an old cowboy on crack, but in a good way."

I held her tighter, breathing deeply, inhaling her sweet scent. "What about me?"

She laid her head on my chest. "You're perfect."

"So right in this moment, nothing else exists? Nothing else matters?" I kissed her temple, giving her back her words from last night when we were in the lake.

Livi tilted her head up slightly. "Nothing."

We continued dancing like that, glued together. Her forehead touching my neck, hands clasped.

Livi had changed me, changed my heart. I didn't mean for it to happen, hadn't planned on any of it. I was falling head over heels for her and there would be no walking away and never looking back. If I was forced to leave Livi, I'd spend the rest of my life looking over my shoulder.

The song ended and I spun her out and brought her back in for a hug. I wrapped my arms around her waist, picking her up, and I placed my forehead head against hers. "I don't want to let you go."

She smiled. "Then don't. Dance with me again."

That's not what I'd meant. I put her down and moved her around the floor for two more songs before we needed a beer break. The whole time I was holding her I was running options through my head.

Maybe I could go see her. Maybe we could meet somewhere. Maybe we could figure this out and end up happily ever after.

I knew now wasn't the right time to ask her, but that didn't mean the words weren't on the tip of my tongue. Allie came barreling toward us and she slung her arms around both of us laughing like a nutjob.

"Will you two come up for air please? I want to take some shots and no one in this joint will let me dance on the table."

I chuckled as I led both girls to the bar. "Can I get a round of shots for these two beautiful ladies please?" The bartender looked Allie and Livi up and down, twice. I fought the urge to punch him. I put my arm around Livi's chest and pulled her back against me while he placed our shots in front of us. Cole came from out of nowhere, grabbed Allie's drink out of her hand, and downed it.

She slapped him upside the head as I rolled my eyes. "Can we get another shot?" All I wanted to do was hold Livi close, dance with her, and tell her how I felt. All I got to do was watch the girls and Cole drink and dance themselves into a frenzy.

Don't get me wrong, I was having a great time and had a really great buzz flowing, but I would have much rather been spending the night next to, and when I say next to I mean inside, Livi.

In seventy-two hours I'd gone from professional partier to professional pansy.

***

After what seemed like hours inside that tiny bar, I was more than ready to head home. I placed my arm along the back of Livi's chair and pulled her ear close to my hungry lips. "Hey, sugar, let's get out of here. They're wasted," I gestured to our group of friends, "and I'm horny."

Livi giggled, and much to my appreciation, clapped her hands to get everyone's attention. "How about we take this party back to the house?"

"Totally. These neon lights are starting to give me a headache." Kasey shielded her eyes, getting to her feet and pulling Bailey up with her.

"If I have to dance with Cole one more time, I might keel over." Allie shoved him to the side and he came dangerously close to falling out of his damn chair.

"Great, then let's go, children." I gestured everyone toward the door, rushing them into the waiting Suburban.

Getting everyone out of there had been much easier than I'd anticipated, and as we rode home, I realized exactly how drunk Cole actually was. He was singing to a Miranda Lambert song, and he knew all the words. I took out my cell and videoed a little.

I was on cloud nine myself. Surprisingly, Bailey had pretty much left Livi and me alone most of the night, letting us dance and flirt to our hearts' content. I was going to talk to Livi when we went to bed, tell her how I felt. How much I wanted to see her again.

Climbing out of the car, I walked slowly behind Cole with my arms out waiting to catch him when/if he fell. When we were safely inside, I couldn't help but laugh. "Okay, buddy. I want you to keep an eye out for any trash cans that might come out and tackle you."

Livi pursed her hips, patting Cole on his back. "I've noticed you have problems swallowing without choking lately. Be careful."

Cole narrowed his eyes. "Fuckers." His mouth turned up into a smirk and my stomach dropped. I knew Cole like the back of my hand. I knew where this was headed, and from across the room there was nothing I could do to stop him. "You've been quite the little fuckers all weekend, haven't you?"

The chatter in the room came to a screeching halt. I don't think anyone even breathed. Bailey turned to Livi, self-righteous hands on her bossy hips. "Livi? What? I thought you said, uh, what's going on?"

I reached for Livi's hand; threading our fingers together, I spoke as quietly as I could. "Sugar, please tell them now. You'll feel so much better and we'll be able to spend the rest of the trip in bed." I expected her to fight me on my request, but instead of anger or pain in her eyes all I saw was calm. Maybe it was all the alcohol, or maybe it was my hand in hers and the promise of one more night together.

Livi took and let out a deep breath. "A while back I caught Patrick having an affair and—"

"Oh my god, you saw us?" Bailey's face was pale, and her hands were shaking.

Holy. Fucking. Shit.

Chapter Twenty-Eight

Livi

The whole room was so silent you could hear the sound of Bailey's ice cubes shaking in her glass. I stopped breathing for a few moments, my pulse thrumming in my veins. Nothing made sense. I felt like I was present and floating all at the same time. It was Kasey gasping that finally made everything come crashing back into focus.

"What? No. I saw him and his... Wait. What? Saw *us*? Like you and him? You slept with Patrick?" My mind was suddenly reeling. I had decided to come clean with my best friends, with the people who knew and loved me most. Of all the people in the world, if anyone had told me Bailey had slept with Patrick, I would've told them they were crazy. "Bailey?"

"Livi, let me explain, please." She had her hands out like she was trying to calm down a crazy person. I wanted to laugh. She hadn't seen anything yet.

Allie, Kasey, and Cole were all sitting side by side on the couch, watching us like a made-for-TV movie. In their defense, they all looked equally distraught.

"Let you explain why you had an affair with my husband? Please, by all means."

"Patrick and I ran into each other at a conference in New York. We were both drunk and lonely and one thing led to another. I am so sorry, Livi. Neither one of us wanted to hurt you and—"

"Lonely? You were both fucking married to other people. Just because you were alone at the conference doesn't mean you were *lonely*. Does Matt know? Does your husband know about you and Patrick?"

Bailey shook her head slowly, her expression completely terrified. "No."

I put my fingers to my temples. I couldn't believe this was happening. I couldn't believe one of my oldest friends had slept with my ex-husband when he was my husband. It was something that happened to other people, it was something that happened to a colleague's cousin and became a cautionary tale. It wasn't something that happened to me and one of my best friends. "How many times?"

She was silent for a few moments and I was almost afraid I was going to have to start screaming in order to get the answers I deserved. Finally, she whispered softly. "A few."

"So you didn't have a one-night stand in a hotel room in New York. You had an affair with my husband. Yet you still found it in you to spend this whole weekend riding around on your high horse giving me shit for flirting with Taylor."

"Liv, I didn't want you to make the same mistakes I did. Matt and I are in counseling. Patrick called me this weekend over and over desperate to talk to you, he said he was afraid he was losing you—"

I cut her off again. "I didn't make the same mistakes you did, Bailey. I would never make those kinds of choices. Taylor and I did nothing wrong. I filed for divorce *months* ago."

Allie stood, putting her hand on my shoulder. "Why didn't you tell us, Livi?"

I shrugged her off. I wasn't mad at Allie, but I needed to get away. I went and stood by Taylor, letting him pull me close. "It's kind of funny when you think about it, really. I didn't tell y'all because I wanted a relaxing weekend where you guys didn't throw a pity party for me over something I've been over for a while. I wanted a weekend when I didn't have to think about infidelity or divorce. A weekend where I didn't have to think at all. I wanted to come here and let loose with my friends." I looked over at Taylor as I squeezed his hand. "Up until five minutes ago, that's exactly what I got."

"Livi, please, we can work through this. We've been friends for so long, please don't stay mad at me." Bailey was all but begging me, for what I wasn't sure. She'd slept with my husband, and I would never be able to unknow that.

"What do you want me to say, that I forgive you? Sure, Bails, I forgive you for fucking my husband. Actually, for real, I'm not mad at you. I pity you." I started laughing a manic laughter that I'm sure made me look certifiable. "You cheated on Matt with Patrick. How disappointing for you. Don't lie. I know what you were expecting from Patrick, what you thought he'd give you. He's nothing like he used to be. That man is gone. The cold, driven, money-hungry shell that's left is terrible in bed." I turned, still holding Taylor's hand like he was my lifeline, and stepped in the direction of our little bedroom.

Then I stopped and faced Bailey one last time. "I'm sad, Bailey. I'm sad that you thought so little of me, of our friendship, and of yourself to do what you did. I thought you were better than Patrick. I know without a doubt that I am."

Chapter Twenty-Nine

Taylor

I followed Livi out onto the porch, closing the door softly behind me when I knew she had wanted nothing more than to slam it. Never in a million years would I have imagined the night would end like it had. Cole was the domino that started an unfathomable chain reaction. It'd warmed my heart when Livi came to me, when she'd needed me out of everyone in that living room. I hurt for her, for what she'd learned, but I also had hope that maybe she would want more from me, like I did from her.

"Livi, baby I—"

"No. All I want for the rest of the night is for you to make me forget. Forget that my best friend betrayed me. Forget that my ex-husband sucks way worse than I thought he did. Make me forget it all, Tay. Can you do that?"

I wanted to hold her and let her talk out her issues. I wanted to be the man who picked up her shattered pieces and glued them back together. I wanted to be her whole world. All she wanted was one more night. One more night with the arrogant playboy who made her come. I mean I was a weekend of fun kind of guy. She didn't want a future with me. I was her great escape. My heart was crumbling at her feet and she had no fucking idea.

I nodded slowly. "Anything you need, sugar, it's yours." I watched as she peeled her top over her head and shimmied out of her shorts. She stepped over to me wearing her lacy black bra and matching panties. Livi started undoing the buttons of my shirt as I reached down and shredded her underwear the way she needed me to. She peered up at me through her long black lashes. I'd told her that I knew she loved it when I did that. The truth was, I loved it too. I loved giving her what she wanted, the slight rough edge to our sex.

We were perfect together. I wished she could see it.

I picked her up and tossed her on the small bed. After removing the rest of my clothes, I covered her body with mine. She spread her legs, her body like a beacon to mine. When she reached between us, grabbing my bare cock and positioning it at her entrance, I froze. "Livi?"

"You said anything I needed."

"I did. But when I brought it up before—"

"Things change, Taylor."

What the fuck did that mean? Things change? The only thing that had changed between then and now was that I was falling for her and she was walking away in the morning.

"I mean, if it's not still okay, I thought—"

"It's still okay." I brushed a stray hair off her forehead. Livi had stolen all the sanity from my brain. Maybe it was because all the blood in my body was constantly pumping down into my dick while I was in her presence. "I want to feel you, god, I want you this way more than I should."

She put her hands on my ass, pulling me deep inside of her. The heat and the sensations, it was almost more than I could stand. "Oh god, baby. You feel so fucking perfect." I needed more. I grabbed her legs, wrapping them around my waist. Pinning me inside of her. I'd never wanted to leave before. Now, I could die right in this moment and it would be the perfect way to go.

I set a slow pace at first, drawing out her pleasure until she was begging me for more, for harder, and faster. She wanted to be dominated, for me to force all thoughts from her mind. I guess in the end, I *was* the man helping her heal, only not exactly in the way I wanted to.

I began to pound into her body, over and over. The headboard was banging against the wall, the bed was squeaking. I had to put one hand on her shoulder to keep her in place.

"Is that what you need, baby? Like that?"

"Oh god, Taylor. So fucking good. Please don't stop."

I was so close to the edge, the sensations were too strong, it was too real feeling her body wrapped around me with nothing between us. I wasn't going to last much longer.

"Come for me, sugar. Come for me, Livi."

Her nails dug into my ass as she screamed my name while her orgasm washed over her. Her muscles clenching and tightening, milking my dick, had me following close behind.

I should've pulled out, but no part of me wanted to. I needed to know she was full of me, that part of me would be inside of her while she slept wrapped in my arms.

Nothing about my feelings for Livi made sense, but I was so fucking far past caring.

Chapter Thirty

Livi

Last night was one of the most difficult and best nights of my life. Dancing with Taylor, laughing, holding him close, had been heaven. Coming home to find out that my best friend had an affair with my ex-husband sucked giant horse balls. Having Taylor take me to bed and nail every thought from my mind also fell in the win column. We slept, tangled up in each other, like we had every night this weekend.

I opened my eyes to sunlight streaming into our tiny sanctuary. I wanted to cry. While I needed to get out of this house and away from Bailey, I was heartbroken about leaving Taylor. I had to leave him behind today and go back to reality. A reality that didn't include him. It'd taken only three days to fall for the arrogant, cocky, hilarious, gorgeous playboy lying next to me. With his arm and leg draped over my body, warming me, protecting me, making me feel safe and wanted. I shifted, which was difficult under the weight of his limbs, turning my body toward him.

His bright blue eyes opened and his face broke into a smile. "Good morning, beautiful."

"Good morning, handsome."

"Handsome? I don't think I've ever been called handsome before."

"Really?"

"Yeah, it's usually sexy, hot, fuckable, you get the picture."

"How about cocky and arrogant? Ever been called those things?"

He laughed quietly, brushing my hair over my shoulder. "A time or two." Then his smile fell. "What time is your flight?"

"I need to be at the airport by noon. My flight leaves at one, Kasey and I are on the same flight."

He turned on his side, facing me. "What about Bailey?"

"Don't know. Don't care." I sighed, rubbing my fingers through his hair. "I'll get over it eventually. Down the road, we'll be amicable, but it'll never be like it was before. The trust is gone. We'll never be the same." I felt my eyes swell with tears. I tried my best to blink them away before Taylor noticed.

He placed his warm hand on my cheek. "Time heals all wounds."

"Hope so. Tell me about you. What's next in the exciting world of Taylor Hill?"

"Well, I'll graduate with a degree I love but will never get to use. I'll start working for my dad's company the week after graduation." He kissed my neck softly. "In the near future, I'll be nursing a broken heart, so that'll take up some solid time on my schedule."

I snorted. "Broken heart my ass."

"I mean it, Livi. Leaving you today is not going to be easy for me."

I wanted to believe him. I wanted Tay to feel about me the way I felt about him. I wanted to find a way we could see each other, be together. I wanted not to have made another mistake falling for the wrong guy.

"Me either."

I didn't say anything about us seeing each other, talking or texting. I wanted to so bad, but my life was still chaotic right now. I had to think of myself, and get myself in order.

Taylor was only now starting his adult life. I didn't want to weigh him down with my issues. He'd be fine. By next weekend, he'd have another girl in his bed, if not sooner.

I was the one who would be nursing a broken heart for a while.

***

Two hours and two orgasms later, Taylor and I finally got out of bed. He didn't bother slipping out the side door, and we wandered into the house together to use the bathrooms and get some coffee. I went back to my porch bedroom and saw Taylor's bag next to mine. He'd been so certain I was a sure thing, or maybe he'd been hopeful. Either way, seeing his bag there made my heart ache.

I packed my stuff and got ready to go home. Seeing everyone else's suitcases by the door made me thoroughly depressed. Apparently, Bailey had gotten up at the crack of dawn and had taken a cab to the airport. She'd switched her flight, probably thinking it would be easier on me if I didn't have to see her today. She was right. I wasn't ready to start dealing with her betrayal. I was grateful for the gesture, even if it protected her as much as it did me.

Allie and Cole were sitting on the couch, harboring hangovers. "Livi Lou, is there any more smoothie stuff? Please help me. I can't fly like this. I'll puke everywhere."

I went into the kitchen and pulled together what I needed, making them each my special hangover cure. "Here you go, you big babies."

Taylor brought our bags out and placed them next to everyone else's. He plopped down in an armchair and playfully yanked me onto his lap, wrapping his arms around my waist and resting his head on my arm.

Kasey came and joined us. "So are we going to talk about it, or ignore it?"

I knew what she meant, and she was right; keeping things inside hadn't helped any of us this weekend. "Well, Bailey had sex with my husband—"

"*Ex*-husband," Taylor interjected.

"Exactly. Thank you, my ex-husband while we were still married. She lied. She cheated. She fucked up. In time, I suppose, I will get past it, but things between us will never be the same. I would never ask you guys to stop talking to her or to treat her differently, but I can't promise that I'll be willing to do another trip with the four of us."

Allie nodded, noisily slurping the last of her smoothie down. "We love Bailey, but we love you too. When she hurt you, she hurt all of us. I want to hate her for destroying what we've had, the trust we shared, but I can't."

I smiled. "I don't want you to hate her, Allie. I don't hate her."

Cole sat up. "I'm really sorry about last night. I feel like a douche."

Taylor rubbed his hands on my bare thighs. "That's because you are a douche."

I shook my head, hoping to reassure him. "Don't be sorry, Cole. Everything happened the way it was supposed to. Who knows if she would have ever told me the truth otherwise?"

We were all quiet for a while, me resting my head on Tay's shoulder, his arms still around me making me feel more conflicted. I wanted to stay with him, but I had to get home, finalize my divorce, and get on with my life.

Cole looked at his watch, wincing. "I hate to be the one to say this, but it's time to go."

Tears threatened, and I willed them away, trying to get my emotions under control. I wouldn't do the sniveling clingy girl in front of Taylor. It was bad enough to feel my heart breaking, I didn't have to broadcast it to the world.

After the guys loaded up all our luggage, we drove the too-short distance to the airport. Kasey was sitting up front with Cole, Allie was stretched out in the third row, and Taylor and I were holding each other in the middle row with me half on his lap.

"Good luck with your finals. Email me and let me know how it goes," I whispered to him.

"Sure. Thanks." He looked out the window and then back to me, jaw clenched. "Livi, I, uh, I really um, shit. Can I maybe call you sometime?"

I beamed like a girl with a schoolyard crush at his stuttered words and what I hoped was the meaning behind them. "I'd like that." I took a deep breath, resting my forehead against his shoulder. "Thank you for everything. I had more fun with you this weekend than I've had in a long time. You're great, you know that?"

"I, uh, I can't even begin to tell you." He was whispering so only I could hear his sweet confession. "I've never met anyone like you before. You are so strong and smart and beautiful. You mean something to me, Livi. You'll always mean something to me. I'm only a phone call away. Or, you know, a flight."

I think I stopped breathing for a second. *A flight?* Was he suggesting we see each other again? I was thrilled at the same time I knew it wasn't a good idea. I was a divorced chick, newly bitter about another one of her ex-husband's affairs. Right now, I wasn't what Taylor needed. I had to pull myself together and find my center. Instead of saying what I wanted to say, which was *I fell for you at some point over the last three days please come see me.*

Please call, email, and text. I said nothing. I simply smiled and laid my head back on his shoulder.

Chapter Thirty-One

Taylor

Livi said nothing. She didn't say fuck off, but she also didn't say sure, I'd love to see you again. She said *nothing*. I didn't know what to do with that. I didn't know if I should try to convince her I was the worth her time, or if I should let her go. Let her go the way I promised her I would before we started this thing between us.

In the end, we rode the rest of the way in a sad silence. I'd never felt dread swim in the pit of my stomach like this before. The closer we got to the airport, the more upset I became. I felt like a fucking pussy, but I didn't care. I wanted Livi, and she was leaving.

Cole pulled the Suburban to the curb, climbing out to get their luggage. I helped Livi out, then stood beside the car, watching her say good-bye to my best friend. She hugged him and gave him a kiss on his cheek, then she walked over to me.

She was so beautiful, and she looked so sad. I figured it had mostly to do with Bailey's betrayal, and maybe a little bit to do with me.

I pulled her close, and whispered in her ear, "Be safe, sugar."

We kissed one last time, and she left. Totally ironic that I talked such a big game, and she was the one walking away in the end.

She never looked back either. Not once.

If she had, she would have seen my knees buckle and my heart shatter.

Chapter Thirty-Two

One Month Later

Livi

Summer was almost over, and my beautiful tan from our weekend at the lake had long since faded. That was what happened when you moped around your house and lived most of your day on your couch watching teen dramas. Then spent the rest of your time writing love stories about people that were real only inside your head.

Kasey had come for a visit to check on me. Every time we talked she said I sounded like death warmed up.

"Livi Lou, you have got to leave this house at some point." Kasey pulled me up off the couch by my arm.

As soon as she let go, I flopped back down like rag doll. "Actually, I don't. I get really healthy food delivered. I hired a personal trainer who comes over three times a week, and all I need to do my job is the internet and a laptop."

"Livi. You've got to snap the hell out of it. This is getting ridiculous. Okay, your ex-husband had an affair with one of your best friends. I get it, you miss Taylor. But, honey, life goes on. The world keeps spinning."

I knew Kasey was right. It's not my divorce or Bailey's betrayal that had left me feeling blah. The divorce was final, and I was glad it was finally done. There wasn't a reason for Patrick to ever contact me again, and damn, didn't that feel great.

Over time, I knew I'd process what Bailey had done in a way I could live with, but I'd lost a friend who I'd never get back.

What had me feeling like I'd been hit by a Mack truck and had all the wind knocked out of me was Taylor. I missed him with every bone in my body, and every beat of my heart.

Kasey read my mind, like only an old friend could. "Why don't you call him?"

"Great idea, Kase. And say what? *Hey, I know I'm divorced now. Do you want to like date me?*" I rolled my eyes. "Come on. He graduated like ten minutes ago. He has his whole life in front of him and that life is in Georgia." I shrugged, looking down at my baggy sweatpants. "Plus, the phone works both ways. He hasn't called me, and I didn't expect him to. He's living his life."

Kasey sat next to me and gave me her *I'm about to lecture you so take it like a pro* look. "You're right Liv, his life is in Georgia. But you know what? Yours is mobile. You said so yourself. All you need is internet and a laptop. Your divorce was final last week. There's nothing holding you here."

I stuck out my bottom lip. "You guys are here."

She shook her head. "No, we aren't. I'm in San Antonio, Allie is in Dallas, and Bailey is, well, Bailey isn't really someone you want to spend time with anyway."

"I know that none of you live *in* Austin. I meant, you're all in Texas. What? You'd have me move to Georgia? I don't think so. That's needy and gross. I'm not uprooting my life for a guy who may not want to see me again." I'd been through one failed marriage. I didn't need to add any more embarrassment to the résumé.

Kasey slapped my thigh, harder than necessary for a friendly pick-me-up. "I wasn't telling you move to Georgia, Livi. That's insane. I meant maybe you should go for a visit." She stared at me and I ducked my head. "Wait. Do you want to move to Georgia? Have you been thinking about it?"

"No." I refused to make eye contact. It wasn't a lie per se. I wanted so badly to be with Taylor again. Feel his hands on me, his gaze tracking my movements, his warm body curled around mine as we slept. "Look, he and I set ground rules before anything happened. We had a weekend fling. No looking back."

"Bullshit, Livi. I heard him at the airport. I heard him all but ask you if he could come see you. You said nothing. The expression on his face was past sad." Kasey mimicked a pouty face.

"I'm no good for him. I have baggage."

"Get over yourself," Kasey snapped then threw her hands in the air. "You don't have baggage. You got divorced from a cheating, lying asshole. Who cares? It happens all the time. Especially when your ex is a lying, cheating asshole. It doesn't mean you're marked as unfit for a relationship for the rest of your life."

I sighed and leaned back into my comfy couch. My new BFF. "What if Taylor doesn't want me?"

"What if he does?"

Stupid Kasey with all her encouragement and logic. "What if he turns out to be bad for me, like Patrick?"

Kasey turned to face me, folding her hands in her lap, calmly ladylike. "Livi, I need to tell you something. This is something I should have told you a very long time ago—"

"Did you sleep with Patrick too?"

"Ew." Kasey snorted, making a *how disgusting* face. "Not a chance in hell. Listen, okay?"

I nodded.

"Patrick was never the man for you. I know you have it all built up in your mind that for a while your life was a fairytale. But it never was, Livi. Patrick never put you first. Not once. He said all the right things, did all the right things to make you fall for him, but he was never your prince charming. I saw you smile and laugh and play more in three days with Taylor than I ever saw you do with Patrick. He never got you, Liv. He wanted you to be less than you were, and it was torture to watch. Patrick being with Bailey, cheating on you more than once, was a blessing in disguise. You're free, Livi, act like it."

I was dumbfounded, shocked, and stunned. "You all hated him? You all knew he wasn't the one for me, but you never said anything? You let me marry him?"

"Oh, Livi Lou." Kasey smiled sadly. "We were a bunch of kids. We were all trying to find our way in this world. You seemed happy, so we were happy for you." She shook my hand, making my whole arm bounce around. "Now we're adults. I'm sitting here telling you that Taylor is the guy for you, he's good for you. You'd be an idiot to let him slip through your fingers." She stood and walked to the other side of the room. "Which is why I called Cole."

"You what?" I screeched.

Kasey nodded and held her hands out in front of her, warning me away. What did she think I was going to do, hit her? She might be right. "I called Cole, well, Allie and I did. We were on speaker phone. Anyway, we told him that you missed Taylor, but were being stubborn."

I shook my head. "I cannot fucking believe the two of you."

"Believe it, sister. We would do any and everything possible to make you happy. Cole said that Tay has been miserable the last few weeks too. He talks about you constantly."

"Really? Cole said that?" I felt my anger dissipate instantly, making me such a silly, stupid girly girl I wanted to smack myself.

"Yep, he did." Kasey walked farther away from me, into my kitchen. Putting the granite island between us. "So, we sent him a ticket to come see you."

"You. Did. Not." Never mind, girly girl gone. My anger was coming back with a vengeance.

"We did." Kasey reached up and grabbed a bottle of wine off my wine rack, uncorked it in record time, then poured me a really full glass. "His flight gets in tomorrow morning."

I grabbed the glass when she handed it to me with an outstretched arm like a peace offering. I downed its contents in twenty seconds. "He's actually coming? You're sure?"

Kasey nodded, a smile on her face. "He's coming. Cole is picking him up in the morning to take him to the airport."

"I don't know if I want to kiss you or kick you."

She shrugged. "The kiddo is at my mom's house for the night. So how about you and I polish off this bottle of wine and watch some chick flicks? We'll keep you company, and calm, until tomorrow."

"We?"

Kasey's knowing smile grew before taking a sip of her wine. "Allie is on her way. She'll be here in an hour or so."

I was speechless and overwhelmed. My friends. The love they had for me was so profound. I knew that, because mine was the same for them. In all my wallowing, I forgot they were the best lifeline I had.

I walked around the counter, put my glass down, and hugged my best friend. "Thank you, Kasey."

"You're welcome, Livi," she whispered as she hugged me back.

Chapter Thirty-Three

Taylor

I'd paced the length of my hotel room at least a dozen times. I'd started about a hundred texts to Livi, only to delete every one of them. I wanted to tell her I was in town and that I wanted to see her, but I was terrified. What if she said no? I'd talked to Cole, who had talked to Allie a few days ago. Apparently they had become buddies. She told Cole that Livi missed me. Her divorce was final, and apparently Patrick was still trying to get her back. I wanted to track that son of a bitch down and kick his ass. I wanted to tell him that she was mine now and he better back the fuck off.

But I didn't because she wasn't. Cole had given me a ticket to come to Austin, he'd basically kidnapped me and put me on the plane. But hell, her missing me didn't mean she wanted to see me. To Livi I was a fling, a good time.

How could I blame her? That's what I told her I was. I was some guy who flirted for a living and went to school because he had nothing better to do. I drank and partied and whored around. I slept too late and I couldn't cook. I didn't even know how to do my own damn laundry. I was a joke. She needed a man. Someone who could provide for her, give her support and stability. Someone to make her life better, not make her life harder.

***

Four hours later and I was still hiding like a chump in my hotel room. I'd procrastinated like a motherfucker. I'd gone down to the gym and worked out. I'd showered, answered work emails, and watched a ridiculously dramatic movie. Now I was sitting on my bed in complete silence with my phone in my hand. It was time to man up. It was time to call Livi and ask if she wanted to see me.

When there was a knock at the door, I hopped up, welcoming the brief distraction. I'd ordered a bucket of ice-cold beer, and really, I should drink a couple before I called her. I needed to get rid of some of these nerves before I got on the phone and made a fool of myself.

I opened the door, and my hearted stopped when I saw who was there. "Livi."

"Hey."

Holy hell.

I couldn't believe she was real and standing in front of me. So close I could reach out and touch her if I weren't such a scared bastard. "I was about to call you. How did you know I was here?"

"Oh, uh, Allie and Kasey talked to Cole. So…"

My god she was even more beautiful than I remembered. Her hair was down and loose, her jeans hugged her ass, and the rip in the thigh was sexy as hell. She always looked amazing without even trying. My heart started to beat again, reminding me that I was alive.

"Livi, I'm so glad you're here."

"Really?"

Now that my head stopped spinning, I noticed how nervous she was. She shifted her weight from one foot to the other and chewed her lip.

"Oh yeah, sugar. You have no idea how much I've missed you. I think about you constantly. I've wanted to call you a thousand times, but I wasn't sure if you wanted to hear from me."

I reached into the hallway, grabbed her hand, and brought her into the room. Having her hand in mine made my blood heat.

"When you were leaving, I told you I wanted to see you again and you didn't say anything. I figured the weekend was over and you were done with me."

She shook her head. "No. Uh…um… I thought, well, I was in the middle of a divorce, and my life was kind of a mess. I figured maybe you didn't need or want the hassle."

I ran my free hand through my hair. "Are you kidding me? You are the best thing that has ever happened to me. You changed me in the best possible way. I've never cared about anyone the way I care about you. You're all I can think about, you consume me. I miss you every second of every day." I pulled her body against mine. "You are good for me, sugar. Too good for me."

"I missed you too, Tay."

"I'm so damn happy that you're standing in front of me right now."

She smiled, sighing like she was relieved that I wanted her as much as she wanted me. "What happens now? I'm in Texas, you're in Georgia and—"

I grabbed her face with both hands and kissed her with everything I had. Then, so very unlike the playboy I was before I met Livi, I pulled away. I left her standing beside the bed I bet she thought I would ravish her on. I walked over to the dresser where I'd left my phone and picked an old country tune from my playlist. I didn't have all the answers, I didn't know exactly what our future would look like, but I did know what should happen next.

"Dance with me?" Livi smiled as I gathered her in my arms, holding her close and moving to the beat. She rested her head on my chest, her scent surrounding me completely. Part of me couldn't believe that she was here, that her body was moving against mine. It was like an actual dream come true. "I'm not letting go this time."

I'd spent three days with Livi, and those three days had altered everything I thought I knew about life, about living. The moment she'd walked out onto the porch wearing my Bulldogs tank top, I'd been a goner. I'd fallen in love so damn fast I'd almost missed it.

No, I was never ever letting her go again.

Epilogue

One Year Later

Taylor

"Sugar, I'm home." I threw my jacket on the bench by the front door, then walked through the living room and into the kitchen. Livi was standing by the stove, phone to her ear. I snaked my hands up her shirt and kissed her neck. I couldn't help myself. It'd been eight hours since I'd seen her.

She laughed when I tickled her ribs. "Kasey, I'm going to have to call you back. My perpetually horny husband is home."

I waited for her to hang up before grabbing her around the waist, setting her on the kitchen counter, and stepping between her thighs. "How's Kasey?"

Livi kissed me, then pulled back before I was ready to let her luscious mouth go. "She's good. She says hi."

I pushed her hair to the side and nibbled on her collarbone. I would never get enough of my woman. "We're still on for the lake house next month, right?"

She moaned and nodded. "Yup. Kasey and her family will be there, Allie and Carson, and Cole and his latest fling." She ran her fingers through my hair, making my eyes roll back in my head. "Which, by the way, Allie told me Cole's chick of the month is a prostitute?"

I scoffed. "She is not a prostitute. She's a model." I loved that Allie and Cole had become friends. Carson, Allie's husband, wasn't a huge fan, but any jealousy was unnecessary. Allie and Cole were like sniping siblings.

Livi snorted out a laugh. "Lovely. Us and another one of Cole's hot little nobodies should be a super-special family vacay."

I smiled against her neck, my tongue darting out to take a quick taste. "Aw, sugar, of course it will be."

I'd gone to Austin a year ago, hoping and praying that Livi would want to see me again. As it turned out, she wanted to see me every day for the rest of her life. The four months of long-distance love had been tough, but once Livi moved to Georgia, everything fell into place. We'd been married for two months now, and each day was better than the last. Her marrying me made me the luckiest man in the world.

"I have a surprise for you."

Livi's smile was perfect as she pulled back to look at my face. "You do?"

I nodded. "Close your eyes."

She cocked her head to the side, studying me for a few seconds. "You aren't going to pull your dick out again, are you?"

"No, sugar. Well, not right now I'm not." She closed her eyes and I took a key out of my pocket and held it in front of her face. "Okay, open them." She looked confused. "It's for the house."

She wrinkled her nose. "Babe, I love you, but giving me a key to the house we already own doesn't really count as a surprise."

I grinned, loving what I was about to tell her. "What about giving you the key to the lake house?"

"Shut. Up," she squealed.

I chuckled when she started raining kisses all over my face. "It's all ours."

Livi took the key out of my hand, shaking her head in disbelief. "How did you even know it was for sale? When I rented it for next month, no one said anything."

"Yeah, well, Bailey called me. She said the owners contacted her and let her know they'd put the house up for sale." I shrugged. "She knew how much that house meant to us."

"Wow. That's really, um, I don't know what to say."

"Maybe you could give her a call sometime?"

She nodded. "Yeah. I don't know. Maybe."

I kissed her mouth, her neck, her chest, and finally her stomach. "Now we can take our little girl to the lake as often as we want."

I'd convinced Livi that we should start trying to have a baby before our wedding, and for reasons I didn't question, she'd agreed. She was now almost four months along, and I swear she got sexier every day.

After I'd graduated, I didn't go to work for my father. I couldn't see myself spending the rest of my life doing something I hated. He wasn't as pissed as I thought he'd be. I guess the gorgeous wife and the grandbaby on the way softened him a little. I wound up getting a job working for the state in their public relations department. Turned out all those years I spent dialing up the charm made me an invaluable asset when it came to convincing people what was good for them, and generally winning over the masses.

Livi and I lived a few hours away from the lake house where we'd first met, and we'd been back more than once. When Bailey called to tell me it was for sale, I knew I had to have it.

I wanted to make so many more memories on that little side porch with my Livi. I wanted endless late-night dips in the lake, and hikes that went around the long way. I wanted to teach our kids how to swim in the pool, and I looked forward to barbequing with Cole on the back porch. I wanted to listen to Allie give him a hard time about the girls he brought around until he finally found his Livi.

I wanted to vacation with my family, the one Livi and I would create all because we met that fateful summer last year. We'd started out promising each other nothing more than a fling, but thankfully, we'd fallen in love.

"This baby could be a boy, you know." She ran her fingers through my hair, snapping me out of my thoughts.

I laughed loud. "Nope. It's definitely a girl. I deserve nothing less than a house full of beautiful daughters. Payback for the womanizing playboy I was until I met you."

I would be fine with daughters.

I would live and die a happy man surrounded by my all beautiful girls.

ABOUT THE AUTHOR

L.P. lives in Austin, Texas with her husband, two daughters, two dogs, and two chickens.

Writer, business owner, and office manager, L.P. says she loves to read as much as she loves to write. Reading a good book is her reward after writing one. In her spare time—ha!—she fosters puppies for a rescue organization based in Austin.

Connect with L.P.:
Website: www.lpmaxa.com
IG: @lpmaxa
Twitter: @lpmaxa
FB: pages/LP-Maxa/1442560722667127

www.BOROUGHSPUBLISHINGGROUP.com

If you enjoyed this book, please write a review. Our authors appreciate the feedback, and it helps future readers find books they love. We welcome your comments and invite you to send them to info@boroughspublishinggroup.com. Follow us on Facebook, Twitter and Instagram, and be sure to sign up for our newsletter for surprises and new releases from your favorite authors.

Are you an aspiring writer? Check out www.boroughspublishinggroup.com/submit and see if we can help you make your dreams come true.

www.ingramcontent.com/pod-product-compliance
Lightning Source LLC
Chambersburg PA
CBHW071314130626

46556CB00004B/1601